BODHI

A.R. HADLEY

ISBN: 978-0-9996527-7-0

Cover Design: Najla Qamber http://www.najlaqamberdesigns.com/

Cover Images: Deposit Photos. Used with permission.

Editor: Monica Black http://www.wordnerdediting.com/

Proofreading: Devon Burke https://www.joyediting.com/

❀ Created with Vellum

for Kate — both of you

"Open his eyes, LORD, so that he may see." — 2 Kings 6:17

1

"She's only had two?" a man asked the bartender as he tipped his head in the direction of Audrey.

She fiddled with the hem of her black A-line dress and the celery in her drink while taking a quick glance at his reflection in the mirror.

Shaved head.

Stubbly beard.

Average height.

His eyes ... she couldn't quite make out their color, and she didn't want to seem like she was trying.

And he was correct.

Audrey *had* ingested two drinks.

The maximum amount allowed.

One of the things clearly listed on the sheet of "rules" posted at the entrance. Maybe two drinks had even been too many tonight. But they'd also been food. Everyone knew a Bloody Mary functioned as both dinner and recreation. Tomato juice plus olives and celery. *Duh.* Liquid sustenance mixed with the few shots of courage she needed to follow through with whatever the evening had up its sleeve.

"Yeah," the bartender replied to the man, seeming not fazed by him in the least as she gave Audrey a smile and a wink.

The bartender's name was Darcy. She had shiny blue hair. And nipple rings she didn't bother disguising. They'd already properly met and shaken hands — the women, not the jewelry. Kate had introduced them. Kate had said she knew practically everyone at Bodhi, but Kate had disappeared — off to a private room with a tall, mysterious, somewhat dark-haired man named Peyton.

Mysterious to Audrey anyway. In the few weeks Audrey had known Kate, she'd told her very little about Peyton.

He likes belts. Has a thing for them. He's my Dom. He's fucking gorgeous.

Well, maybe Kate had mentioned a few things.

"Tell her to finish up and then call an Uber," the man said, pressing his damn hands into the bar top, the slightest dusting of dark hair on his knuckles grabbing her attention as he leaned forward and scanned the shelves.

The impertinent man still hadn't so much as turned his head when speaking to Audrey — no, *about* her — as he eyeballed everything around her and beside her and across from her.

"Excuse me?" Audrey perked up and stopped fiddling with the items she'd made into props and looked at him.

After pushing her long, dirty-blonde hair behind her shoulders, she hoped she also tossed him an eyeful of gumption. She would no longer tolerate this third-person bullshit.

Darcy smirked — Audrey was satisfied she'd amused *someone* — and made her way down the long, lonely stretch of bar. Ornate stools with armrests were tucked under the countertop. Several antique mirrors of various shapes and sizes hung on the walls. Wrought iron hooks were placed studiously by the double doors, ready for coats, rain jackets, or umbrellas.

The action Kate had spoken about obviously happened

somewhere else. This area was a ghost town. And it had been empty when Audrey first entered, nervous and out of her element but ready for a night of observation. An evening to learn how to loosen her grip. Every third Saturday was free and open to the curious public.

"Have you had the tour?" the man asked as he released the death grip he had on the bar top.

He stood tall — yeah, about six feet, *but not fucking average* — and swung his shaved head in her direction.

"Have you watched yet?" He eyed the red ribbon tied about her bicep.

In addition to the coat hooks near the door, there was also a bouncer-type dude who sat behind a desk, gathering information and handing out and overseeing a selection of ribbons.

Black: Dom looking for a sub.
White: sub looking for a Dom.
Gray: Switch looking for a play partner.
Red: Looking. Only looking, observing. No touching. No propositioning. No playing.

The man who asked all the questions finally settled his gaze on Audrey's, meeting her chestnut eyes.

Full on.

Without flinching.

And she wished he hadn't.

She wished he'd kept his stare confined to the wall, Darcy, the full bottles of alcohol. She even longed for the impolite third-person conversation.

Instead, she locked onto the blue of his eyes. The color matched her favorite pencil. The one she kept in stock for projects — a whole selection of blues she'd bought that came in one of those fancy artist's tins. *Prismacolor* claimed it, but this man owned it, created it, sharpened it.

And she couldn't remember the fucking name of it...

"No," Audrey said in reply to his former question. Under the thumb of his sharp gaze, her voice became subdued. She no longer felt a trace of a buzz, not from the alcohol anyway.

The man cocked his head and studied Audrey, looking her over as though she were a sculpture in a museum, examining her shapes and ridges, her imperfections and advantages, while he ran a hand over his scruff. It was dark and sprinkled with a few shards of almost-camouflaged gray. Maybe a few days of stubble. Maybe less. She loved the feel of a man's unshaven face against her cheeks, her thighs.

It had been a long fucking time...

Maybe being at a sex club — shit, not a sex club, a dungeon — wasn't such a stellar idea.

"Who brought you?" he asked with a leftover curtness in his tone she continued to find herself attuned to. Every nerve in her body vibrated like a perfectly plucked instrument whenever he spoke.

Darcy reappeared and took Audrey's glass even though it still had a few delicious drops of Bloody remaining. Darcy also answered for Audrey, because the cat — or the man with the blue eyes and intense stare — had gotten her tongue.

And the pencil ... it's Copenhagen blue! The color of Van Gogh's *The Starry Night.*

"Kate," Darcy answered for Audrey, gifting them another wink, her violet eyes shining through the lenses of her Buddy Holly glasses.

"Come with me," he said, gesturing toward a set of doors.

His black T-shirt couldn't conceal the heft of his arms, and Audrey wanted to run her hands across his biceps or press her nose against the outline of muscle there. Probably not what he had in mind at this kind of club. Unless his kink was noses pressed against muscle or he had a hand or nose fetish.

After glancing at Darcy, Audrey shifted her gaze to the anything-but-average man with the shaved head, scruffy face, and colored-pencil eyes. The bartender nodded her approval, but Audrey still hesitated.

"I don't know your name."

"Gavin," Darcy replied with another fucking wink as the man scowled.

He managed to look both innocent and dangerous — a beautiful combination.

Unable to keep a smile at bay, Audrey stood and followed but remained glued to his side as he led her through the large, wooden double doors and past two open areas where all kinds of decadent things were happening...

A few women and a couple men were being used as foot-stools and drink holders. Several were sucking cocks. One woman sucked multiple cocks, one after another. People watched the cock sucking while talking amongst themselves. And there was surely a host of other activity Audrey wasn't able to observe — or maybe she only noticed what interested her most. And then there were the crosses: St. Andrew's Crosses.

Two in the first open room. Two in the next. Two empty. Two with people strapped on being beaten and touched, slapped and tickled. Tools were being used Audrey didn't have time to label.

Screaming and moaning and the scent of arousal permeated the air — other things Audrey managed to absorb on the brisk stroll to God knew where as they window-shopped for things she couldn't have even dreamed up.

And then they stopped in front of a door. The first of what looked like six at the start of a wide hallway.

She could hear Kate's beautiful moans.

Kate Tracy. Audrey's new friend and accomplice, the one

she'd recently met online who'd brought her into this forbidden world of fetish. And despite thinking otherwise for many, many months, now that the moment had arrived, Audrey wasn't sure she was ready to watch. The blood-red ribbon on her bicep indicated she was there to watch but not participate. It meant she was possibly a BDSM virgin, when, in fact, she wasn't — not totally — but she'd never watched.

Not in the flesh.

She'd imagined it but was now terrified the reality of seeing her friend naked, splayed out, maybe bruised, maybe having an orgasm — she was afraid the reality might crush the dream.

The door had a magnetic dry-erase calendar affixed to it. Kate and Peyton's time slot were written in red. Gavin tapped a code on the panel of numbers to the side, and when the heavy, white metal door opened, the man inside paused and looked over his shoulder.

Once Peyton saw it was Gavin, he only smiled and continued as if nothing had occurred — as if people weren't in the room with them now ... Kate nude and hanging from a contraption attached to the ceiling.

Gavin brought his fingers to his lips, indicating Audrey not speak, and then he pulled her aside near a wall — *to watch* — holding her back against his chest as he wrapped an arm around her neck. It wasn't a romantic overture or means to snuggle.

His grip looked like a chokehold — without the choking.

It was clearly a gesture meant not only for Audrey, but for the man beating Kate and for the onlookers who stood scrunched at the outside of the windows — the people who appeared drunk on expression, hazed and dazed with the anticipation of an orgasm — theirs or his or hers. It didn't matter.

Kate was blindfolded. Her coal-black hair was tied in a high ponytail. The man, Master Peyton, continued to strike her with an ornate leather belt folded in two. Dark tan, long and thick (the belt), and engraved.

Kate was already covered in bruises. Her ass and thighs were welted, red, tinged with superficial wounds. She openly sobbed, though quietly. Tears cascaded down her cheeks, past her mouth, from under her blindfold. She seemed unaware there had even been a disturbance in the room.

After several more lashes, the man holding the implement of destruction and appropriation inserted three fingers inside Kate and said, "There's a man watching you."

Peyton had spoken hypnotically, as if he were waking Kate from a dream. Maybe she'd fallen down the rabbit hole and he'd reached an arm into the dirt to pull her out.

"Kate," Peyton whispered. "Kitten."

"Mmm," she moaned.

"There's a man watching you," he repeated, the same sinister delight in his tone, a devious smile playing across his lips.

"Men at the window," she mumbled.

"No, Katy Kitten. The men at the window are outside. *He* is in the room with us."

Kate sucked in a breath, and as she did, Peyton removed his fingers and struck her again. This time, she cried out, but she didn't ask him to stop.

"You will come," he grunted, fully clothed, an erection straining his blue jeans. His brown bangs — the color appearing to have been kissed by a burnt sunset — lay matted across his sweaty forehead.

"Yes," Kate replied without reservation, adding the word *sir* after a slight pause. A smile formed on her pretty pink lips. She licked at the leftover tears that had rolled down her cheeks.

The grip Gavin had on Audrey's neck tightened. He nipped at her ear, breathed against her skin and hair, causing her knees to buckle, then he pulled her taut again.

"Shhh," Gavin whispered, and Audrey relaxed into him, her body shape molding to his as though they'd taken this position a million times.

His voice felt and sounded full of a foreign but welcome sensuality. It had weight and depth — a much needed rain. She could feel his dick against her back and his breath on her nape.

Peyton took a toy from the table beside him, switched it on, and inserted it into Kate's heat. As he fucked her with the vibrator, he belted her ass with renewed courtesy, alternating the deeds. The sounds she made bled into a symphony.

"Please. Please. Please."

"Please what, Kitten?" Peyton said as he paused.

"Use me," she whispered.

He increased his ministrations without missing a beat, keeping the toy on and the belt poised, rumbling toward a spastic conclusion.

"Come," Peyton demanded, speaking with such richness Audrey thought she might also release.

Her vicarious position, Gavin's hot breath on her skin — his dick against her back, his arm about her neck, clutching her superficial sensitivities — made it a distinct possibility.

"He's here?" Kate asked between pants.

"Yes." Peyton swatted her one final time.

The belt made a loud noise as the stainless-steel buckle hit the floor, and Kate made an even louder noise as she freed what sounded like a mind-blowing orgasm. Audrey could feel the convulsions without seeing Kate's eyes, feeling her friend's pleasure wash over the room like a gentle wave kissing the shoreline.

Peyton unbound Kate, kissed her cheeks, and praised her over and over. "My good, Katy Kitten. Good. Good. Good."

2

After exchanging quiet words with Peyton while Kate kept her blindfold on, Gavin led Audrey out and down the hall.

The new room they entered was much like the one they'd just left. Not much decoration, no fuss. The size of a small hotel suite. But this room was windowless, darker, colder. It had a bed in the center, tools hanging on the walls, and two other closed doors, not including the exit. Perhaps a bathroom and a closet. The only bold colors came from the black leather furniture and the beautiful black-and-white quilt — embroidered with what appeared to be fertility symbols — lying atop the king-sized bed.

The room had been created for a purpose.

Gavin told Audrey to take a seat on the small couch. He retrieved a bottle of water from a mini fridge, instructed her to drink it, then made his way to the door.

Instead of sitting, Audrey followed him, but as he turned and caught her eye, it was clear she wasn't meant to do so. He indicated the couch, utilizing only a stern look in the drowning blue of his eyes.

"Where are you going?" she asked.

He stood inches from her. It was the first time she picked up on his ethereal scent without competition from the bar and the sex and the sweat in all the other parts of the club. She detected cedar and leather and shadows.

"Of all the things you could ask, and you want to know where I'm going?" He stroked a single finger down her cheek.

Audrey had no doubt he was aware of the power he already held over her. A chill passed through her from head to toe.

"I have on a red ribbon."

"Yes."

"You're not my Dom."

He lifted an eyebrow, and he looked sexy even when puzzled. "Say what you mean." He folded his arms across his chest, and she had to concentrate to keep her eyes on his face and not his biceps.

"I think I just did."

"Are you aware you're in a room I will lock you inside of once I leave? And are you aware you haven't told me your name?"

Audrey's face heated, and she dropped her gaze.

"Look at me," he said before she could state her name. "Don't ask questions that produce no consequence. Don't state facts to find what you desire. Simply speak your needs. We have open communication here."

She found that a little unbelievable. Maybe because she'd never had that before: open communication and full disclosure. She was thirty-five, and she didn't think anyone had ever asked her what she wanted.

Saying nothing, she only stared at the inscrutable expression on his soft yet hard-lined face. He appeared not much older than her but seemed to have lived a lifetime.

"What's your name?"

"Audrey."

"Do you have a safe word?"

Her cheeks flushed again. "No."

"Pick one," he commanded, obviously ignoring the red tie he'd already espied about her arm. "I prefer to step outside the standard: red, yellow, green."

"King."

"King," he repeated.

"Yes."

"Yes, what?"

"Yes, sir."

She hadn't known just how much she'd needed the *sir* until it passed her lips — the comfort and certainty it provided. Had he noticed how she breathed easier after it fell from her lips ... as though she'd always said it? It was as natural as *yes* or *no* or *please* and *thank you*. She wished she hadn't waited almost two years to finally create an online account, to meet someone like Kate and others like her. Why had she waited so long to go out in public with fellow kinksters?

She knew the reasons. Two very good ones. Perhaps a third. She'd needed some time. And now she was glad the moment had finally arrived.

"Good girl." A smirk lit his eyes as he nodded. "What do you want?"

She eyeballed him while biting her tongue.

"You thought you would get out of answering? It wasn't a rhetorical question. Speak your needs."

Cheeks heating to a boil, trying to hold back a smile, she lifted her chin and responded with a veil of confidence. "You, sir."

Time passed. The room spun. But he didn't seem affected by her declaration. In fact, he made her wait longer for his next words.

"Are you wearing panties?"

"Yes," she choked out.

"Remove them. Only remove the panties, and then go sit on

that chair." He dipped his head in the direction of a rather large, black leather chair that looked lonely ... perhaps it was missing its ottoman.

Things need each other. Yin needed yang. She needed a dick in her pussy.

Doing as he instructed, she took off her panties and sat, and within seconds, he was there, poised in front of her like a base-ball catcher, prying each of her legs over the arms while she fidgeted, attempting to escape.

"Audrey, say your word anytime, but don't fight me. Relax." Gavin looked at her exposed skin as he pushed the material of her black cashmere dress to her waist, not tearing his eyes from her body.

He didn't look at her face.

His eyes landed on her cunt, and they stayed there. He said nothing, only stared. His eyes, dark and fixated, seemed to speak for him: *Your cunt is fucking beautiful. I will worship you. I will fuck you up and break you, but then I will worship you.*

Gavin spread her lips and examined every part of her pussy while Audrey tried desperately to allow it. She tried to stop trembling. Then he took his hands away and stood, replacing his fingers with a thumb, touching it to the tipity-tip-tip of her swollen, aching little nub.

Audrey gasped. He didn't press though. Didn't make an indentation. She barely knew his thumb was there. It was a whisper of his intention. It was a threat of what was to transpire. A gentle transaction before the damage occurred.

He met her eyes with a danger in his starry-night gaze that hadn't existed moments ago.

"I want to hurt you," he said with a pained authority. "You've played before?" He glanced at her ribbon, his face becoming placid again. Stoic.

"Not with anyone in the lifestyle."

"With a partner?"

"A husband."

"Husband?"

"Ex-husband."

"Did he command you do things to please him?"

"No."

"Did he restrict your breathing?"

"No."

"Burn you?"

"No."

"Did he strike you?"

"He spanked me."

"Hard enough to leave bruises?"

"No," she replied with a strange shame for what her husband hadn't been able to provide creeping up the back of her neck, prickling her skin, heating her. He had been one of the reasons. The third.

"Did you want him to leave marks? Give you orders? Did you want him to make you cry?"

She nodded. "I wanted... Yes. I want to cry ... and scream. I want to hurt. I want to be ... pushed." She didn't break eye contact.

His thumb remained on her clit throughout the conversation. Not pressing, only lying on the precipice of her undiscovered kingdom.

"I will make you scream and cry."

Not can or may. *Will.* She released several years' worth of repressed breaths, then whimpered as she lost contact with his thumb.

He smeared the dampness across her mouth, the smell of her arousal making her squirm.

"Lick," he said with a glint in his eyes.

Opening, she didn't just taste, she sucked, savoring what he offered and wanting more of the tang of her own cunt. She'd never felt so humiliated — spreading her legs for a stranger. She'd also never felt more turned on. Heat had pooled in her belly, dripped through her veins, and swam in her thighs.

After removing his finger, he gave her a tight smile, and then made his way to the door.

"Where are you going?"

She hadn't realized she'd asked him a question, and the same stupid fucking question at that, until the words passed her lips. He answered it anyway, in his own way, without chastising her or embarrassing her.

"You will stay in the chair ... spread. You may touch yourself, but you cannot come. Do you understand?"

"Yes," she exhaled, eager to comply.

"Yes?" he asked with a stern raise of an eyebrow.

"Yes, sir," she replied, and then he exited the room.

Dropping her head against the leather seat, she watched the ceiling. The knockdown took shape. The blobs came to life until her eyes blurred, and she again focused on her body, her nudity, the hollowness she felt between her legs. She stroked herself a moment, rubbed the fuck out of the little nub he had refused to properly entertain. And then she stopped, wishing to do as he commanded. The denial of orgasm resulted in a deep-seated ache ... for him — a stranger who had disregarded her red ribbon.

She needed him to return.

She needed his commands.

Being here with him, listening to him, had taken her mind to the brink of some sort of trance.

And physically, her cunt had never felt so empty.

When he reentered, he seemed the same. He carried nothing but the same neutral expression, displaying only mild interest on his face.

"Did you touch yourself?" he asked as he removed his belt from its loops.

"Yes, sir."

"Did you come?"

"No, sir."

"I'm not going to hurt you the same way Peyton hurt Kate. I won't leave marks anyone can see. These marks will be only for you and me." She nodded. He continued. "I'm a sadist. Do you know what that means?"

"You enjoy inflicting pain for pleasure."

He smiled, almost laughed. "I didn't mean for you to recite the clinical definition. I want to know if you understand what it means for you and me. For this moment, and the next, if you desire."

"Tell me."

"Some have called it a sickness," he began, and she wondered if his words were a test. "It can be perceived as immoral — unethical when it's without boundaries." He paused, raising a proverbial eyebrow. "I have limits. Rules. Things I don't wish to do. But I inflict any type of pain or humiliation I deem necessary, and I take great pleasure in it. Sometimes the pleasure is the pain. An orgasm on the heels of many orgasms can be overstimulating. It hurts worse than those bruises you saw on your friend, and it all makes me harder, makes my desire stronger. It pleases me. Humiliation..."

He stopped, letting the word hang in the air as he folded the belt and touched her pussy with the soft leather. Audrey felt relieved at the contact, even more relieved that he seemed pleased by her reactions thus far.

She hadn't come. She'd stayed seated in the chair. She'd remained spread. And she'd told Gavin what she wanted. Very simply but not nearly the scope of truth.

She needed everything he had to offer — even if it wasn't on the menu.

And she wanted it even more.

"Not all the rooms have windows. A few are private. But people like to watch. Do you like to watch people fuck and bruise, Audrey?" He lifted the belt from her sensitive area, then placed it there again, tapping it to her mound. When he said her name though, she nearly choked on her own spit, unable to take her eyes from him.

"I could feel your pulse in that room with Kate. I felt your breath quicken."

"I haven't..." She stumbled over her words.

"Do you want to watch? It's a simple question."

Audrey nodded.

"People will want to watch you. Like this," he said, indicating her position, her nudity, her supposed humiliation. Her clit pulsed at the forbidden insinuation. "If you were my submissive, I could bind you to this chair while you lay exposed to the windows, the eyes. Every cock would want to be in your cunt, and the women would want to strap on cocks just to crawl inside you. I'd beat you in front of them. Hurt you. Then I would fuck you."

He stopped talking.

Had he?

Audrey's heartbeat sounded in her ears, increasing in intensity. If she did some Kegels, maybe ten or five or three, she'd come, fucking explode with her legs over the arm of the chair without a single one of his fingers on her. His words had been enough to expose her secrets, unlock her desires. This man would or could lead her down a path of hedonism she might never recover from.

He tapped the leather to her exposed flesh — harder than at first — and she flinched ... wanted more.

"Place your arms behind your head. Don't let go," he ordered, and then he swatted her without mercy.

The belt stung her lips and nicked her clit. He did it again without waiting for her to recover. Each time she closed her legs involuntarily, he spread them and smacked her without a word. She winced, cried out, bit her lip. He struck the belt to her pussy again and again. And even though her legs closed, the rest of her never moved. She never tried to get away, never uttered *king*.

Her hands remained clasped behind her head, and her ankles hooked over the arms. The stinging was a remnant — breadcrumbs leading to the ache, the swelling building between her legs.

She panted through the new sensations. And then he stepped away, out of her sight. Too weak and running on endorphins to care, she shut her eyes, only opening them when she smelled his cedar, leather, and sweat return.

A stainless-steel spoon was in his hand. He merely pressed it lightly to her seam, and she jumped.

"Shhh," he said, soothing her. "It's cold?"

"Uh-huh," she replied, unable to form a coherent, adult-like reply.

He pulled it forward like a slingshot, then released. The moment the cold, hard metal made contact with her already swollen seam and clit, she cried out — fucking screamed — and turned her head to the side, wishing he couldn't see her degradation or the pain she felt climbing the walls of her face. But then she realized he needed it — he wanted to see every line of hurt she manifested.

As she met his Copenhagen eyes, the two of them joined in a silent accord. A prayer.

He rubbed the stainless-steel utensil up and down her wet crease, and with each slide, she panted like an animal in heat. She began to heave. She needed to beg. The experience was almost as religious as giving birth. Her legs spread. The sweat. The need to push stronger than almost any other primal instinct known to man.

The mother *had* to push.

Couldn't wait.

And then there was *this* need. And Audrey needed. She needed so much she couldn't even verbalize all of it. But Gavin knew what she needed before Audrey did. It was on the cusp of his tongue, in the skill of his hands. In the way he planned each move.

"You may come," he said, and she sagged, then made a garbled sound. "And when you do, say my name. Not *sir*. My name. And tell me you like to hurt."

He penetrated her eyes with his gaze, watching her as though she were a beautifully broken doll he needed to mend. He could crush the doll, destroy her, then put her back together, and everything would be right again.

"I like to hurt," she burst out.

The orgasm built. He flicked her nub while sliding the spoon through her folds, and then he fucked her with it, repeating the action until she said his name in broken spurts along with the words, "I like to hurt. I like to hurt. Please make me hurt, Gavin..."

She hadn't even finished pulsating when he dropped to his knees in front of her and put his tongue on her bruised and possibly bleeding clit — she couldn't see it, but oh how she wanted to. He sucked it gently, licked it while she squirmed. But the moment she grabbed his face, he stopped.

"Hands back behind your head," he ordered, and she complied.

He began again. But the wiggling resumed. The word *no* fell from her lips like a mantra. Her ass slid against the seat. She tried to inch away.

He grabbed her chin, held it, and shook it. "Have you never had multiple orgasms?"

"No."

"Never?"

"I've touched myself after, but I've never come in succession."

"Then this time, your pain will be from pleasure. And you will take it. You won't touch me or move anymore. And when you come, *and you will come*, you will say my name again. Do you understand?"

"Yes, sir."

"You will come for me." He licked her seam, shoved his tongue into her center, then he took it back to her clit. Hole to seam to clit.

The pleasure couldn't have been measured with all the rulers in the world. The sensitivity had her near bursting. She didn't think she could obey his edict.

"Relax." He licked her softly, teasing her bud with his tongue. "Shhh," he whispered, burying his nose in her folds. "Let it happen. Don't fight me. You're powerful, Audrey. Your body is telling you things. Listen to it."

He licked, sucked, pushed two fingers inside her. She could hear the sounds they made together: his fingers and her cunt. The squishing, the squelching, the wetness.

"Look. Watch."

Lifting her head, she took note of his hooded eyes, the vein in his neck, the stretch in his pants, and then she looked at where they met.

His fingers.

Her cunt.

"Come again," he hissed. "Please me. Say my name."

Bones turning to liquid, she shook over the whole of his

mouth, his fingers, his face, and cried out the name of the man she'd only just met ... without shame.

"Gavin, Gavin, Gavin..."

He stood before she finished, without wiping her juices from his face, and took his dick in hand. "Legs down. Feet on the ground. Eyes here." He indicated his face.

His pants were slung low on his hips, his shirt still on, as he positioned her the way he wanted in the large leather chair. He placed a knee on the cushion next to her waist and a foot on the other side, leaving his hard cock inches from her face.

"Open your mouth."

Still contracting, barely breathing, she tilted her head upright and tried to focus.

"Open your fucking mouth," he said, tapping the head of his cock to her lips. "Lick."

She tasted the precum, dipped her tongue into the slit, wiggling it, and then ... she wanted more. Had to have more. Seized with only the basest of instincts, she inched her head forward and reached for him, but he pulled away and smirked.

"I control this too, baby girl. I will fuck your mouth, and you will allow me all the way inside." He slapped his cock against her cheek. "Yes?" He slapped her other cheek.

"Yes, sir," she replied, then left her mouth open in invitation.

He slipped his cock past her teeth, then pulled it out slick with her spit. He slapped her cheek with it again, tapped her tongue with the tip and asked, "You want my dick, baby girl?"

She made incoherent sounds as he gripped her hair, yanking her face up. Tears flooded her eyes.

"Beg," he growled.

"Please." She stuck her tongue out, trying to lick him. "Please ... fuck my mouth."

Groaning, he shoved himself all the way in, then out, gripping her hair in tandem, ruthlessly penetrating her face while she gagged, resisted, made gurgling sounds ... and then he pulled out.

"Do you want me to stop?"

"No."

"Snap your fingers if you want me to stop. I won't cut off your breathing, but you will gag on my dick. You will retch like a little cock-sucking bitch, and each time you do, it will please me beyond anything you can imagine."

He didn't realize all she could imagine.

She'd imagined filthy, filthy things practically every time she lay beneath her husband. Being used and abused, being taken and fucked, treated like a dirty little whore. Her husband had been a lover, not a fighter, a gentleman, not a Dominant. He couldn't understand, and eventually, she'd lost him to needs she couldn't even articulate at the time. Their communication hadn't been truly *open*. Their love had waned in time.

Oh ... she could imagine...

And she wanted to wrap her mind so far inside Gavin's desire and demands she'd drown.

"Relax your tongue. Relax," he said, pushing himself all the way in, deep into her throat, causing her to gag immediately.

Her eyes watered. She thought for sure she'd vomit, but she didn't as she swam in sensations, the trance. Nothing was in her mind. It was blank. Only delicious cock filled her thoughts and her throat, penetrating her until she couldn't breathe or think or make reason of sense. All she had to do was be open, become a vessel, allow him entrance inside her vulnerability — allow him to attempt to humiliate her with those awful retching sounds.

His hand remaining fixed to her hair, he would occasionally pull out, allowing her to breathe, each time asking if she was okay, but then he would proceed more insistently than before, causing her to gag over and over and over.

And then on what was to be the final withdraw, he said, "Stick out your tongue. All the way."

With the ferociousness of a beast, he pumped himself while she watched, and then he spilled his load onto her tongue and into her mouth, making sure it dribbled down her chin. Leaning back, he smiled, swiped a towel off the chair she hadn't realized he'd placed there, and wiped his cock.

"If you were mine, I'd walk you out there in front of everyone with my cum dripping from the corners of your mouth," he said with a sly grin as he wiped some from the sides of her lips with his thumb. "Would you humiliate yourself further for me?"

She swallowed more of him, then said, "This"—she licked his taste from the corners—"is a privilege." Her eyes darted back and forth as she took stock of the anything-but-average man. "It only humiliates a woman who doesn't feel it's an honor to have received it."

He had no answer for that, or he kept it to himself. Only another smile took shape ... a genuine one. She had pleased him — reached some part of him he seemed to keep closed off. He wiped the rest from her mouth with the towel and asked if she could stand.

They stood eye to eye, Audrey looking up at him from her height of near five-eight, for several intense seconds, her muddy browns to his Copenhagen blues. Then he surprised her by cupping her face and pressing his lips to hers.

"Kiss me," he mumbled, mouth grazing hers. "Show me how you kiss. You lead."

Seeking out his hidden places, she slipped him her tongue, passing any remaining semen to him as she licked him, nibbled him, ate him, tasting him as long as he allowed ... which wasn't long enough.

After pulling away, he met her eyes and told her they would go to Kate. He would see to it both women made it home safely.

But first, Audrey would follow him through the halls. Behind him this time. She wouldn't touch him, and she wouldn't make eye contact with anything but his feet and the floor. He removed her red ribbon and assured her the throngs of people would know by her walk and posture that she belonged to him, she couldn't be shared without his permission, and that she was safe and under his protection.

Except ... he hadn't claimed her, hadn't asked or demanded any formal submission, and still she obeyed him without question. She followed him to Kate — head bowed, novice ribbon removed — without touching him but bound to him.

Kate lay on a tiny sofa, the same type of couch as in the other room sans the color. Everything in this pocket of the world was white. The door. The chair. The tables. The blinds on the windows now drawn to keep the hazy eyes off the aftercare.

Kate certainly seemed to be receiving the treatment. Wearing a fluffy bathrobe, a *white* one, she glowed. Her inky hair was now down and hitting her collarbone A glass of champagne filled her hand, and rosiness brightened her cheeks. However, a different color painted her shoulder blade where the material had slipped, where it looked like Peyton had sunk his teeth into her skin.

Audrey eyed the bruises and marks, and Kate noticed, smiled, and lifted the fleece, then she attempted to stand.

"Sit, Kate," her Dominant said from behind her in the voice of a satisfied grizzly bear.

Peyton may have sounded like a bear, but he wasn't imposing. Thin, lean, and lanky, but not awkward, he stood a couple inches taller than Gavin. His hair was only inches shorter than Kate's, but it was much lighter and had sun-kissed sienna highlights. They appeared natural, though. And he'd replaced his belt with another it seemed.

Peyton always wore a different belt. *Always,* Kate had said.

Audrey didn't normally notice banal things like designer clothing, shoes, or accessories ... on men anyway. However, "things" like belts — the textures, colors and smells, the type of hide — no longer seemed inconsequential.

Nothing in the dungeon seemed frivolous or without thought or merit. Each act was choreographed, timed. Each instrument chosen wisely. This world had been deeply contemplated, then orchestrated.

The smell of the leather must've been an aphrodisiac because Audrey could feel a need rising again, starting in her mind, shooting sparks to her groin. Stealing her gaze from Peyton's waist and one-of-a-kind belt, Audrey's eyes landed on the faces of the men — Gavin's and Peyton's.

As she peered at them, studied them, she felt words passing between them without sound. It seemed something they did often. Communicate with their eyes and their posture. *This place must thrive on ESP.* Darcy, Peyton, and Gavin (the man whose cock she'd swallowed without bothering to ask for a surname) all seemed to speak in riddles using looks and body language.

"Champagne," Kate offered, breaking Audrey's hypnotized stare.

"*We can drink*?" Audrey asked with a stunned blink.

As Gavin held up a finger — one single finger — Peyton smirked. Audrey sat next to Kate and tugged at the robe. Kate, never seeming overly modest or ashamed, let it slip to her waist, exposing her huge breasts and the evidence she wasn't an amateur in the world of BDSM.

The bruises had colored. The welts risen. It hurt a little to look at them — the way it hurt to look at the sun — but Kate's face told a different story. A tale of peace. And just as we needed the sun's light and constancy despite its risk, Kate needed the bruises. They were badges of honor — hippie bullshit in the middle of a fucking BDSM dungeon — and Audrey had a fucked-up clit to prove it.

Bodhi... Maybe it wasn't flower-child bullshit after all.

Kate drank champagne and eased back against the seat and ice.

"You're beautiful," Audrey said with tears in her eyes she couldn't hide, then she kissed the bite on Kate's shoulder.

Gavin came up beside them, wearing a smile, and sat on the arm.

"You were here." Kate popped a small strawberry into her mouth.

"I was. Audrey was too." He tipped his head, his eyes a laser beam of blue, traveling between Audrey and Kate — a straight fucking line of deadly heat a person shouldn't dare under-estimate.

Kate glanced at Audrey, then covered her mouth, but the shit-eating grin escaped. "God, my orgasm was ten times better. No offense, Peyton—"

"—none taken—"

"—but you don't visit the rooms anymore. Unless there's a problem. I almost came when Peyt told me. And *you* were here too." Kate eyeballed Audrey. "I would've liked it if you would've scened with us."

"Really?" Audrey asked, knowing she must've been blushing the color of the berries.

"Yes."

"Well..." Audrey sighed, the uncertainty she'd felt before was being replaced with vigor. "I'm glad we're getting this out in the open."

"Open communication," Gavin interjected.

Kate cleared her throat. "Then time to fess up, *old friend*. Did you two play tonight?" She pointed a finger between Audrey and Gavin. "I see my buddy no longer has her ribbon."

"Yes," Gavin answered, looking at Audrey — no, through her, burning her face with the fire in his eyes. The hollow remained between her legs though.

"Holy fuck," Kate exhaled on a dramatic sigh.

"What?" Audrey asked as Gavin redirected his warm gaze toward Peyton. The men exchanged some sort of James Bond-type espionage in their glances. They seemed to own the fucking patent on it.

"Kate, Kitten, you need to sleep. Those pills should be working soon. Gav will call a driver for you. For both of you," Peyton said without patronization.

"I have my own car," Kate retorted. "We booked a room."

"Someone will drive you to your hotel and bring you back here in the morning for your car. I have your keys," Gavin said, patting his pocket. "I'll return them when you are rested and *not* drinking champagne."

"I've had *one* glass. What? Do you think you *own* the place?" Kate grinned but then gave into his demands. Peyton helped her stand.

"Show me your bruises," Kate gushed to Audrey, but she looked at Gavin as he smirked.

"You dirty devil. What the fuck did you do to her?"

"Kate, now, now..." Peyton began, "bruised ass or no bruised ass, when you use your filthy mouth, you know I might take you over my knee."

"Some bruises are for the inside, Katharine." Gavin kissed the tip of her nose, then he kissed Audrey's.

He took hold of Audrey's shoulders, squaring them, and sighed, but he kept his gaze on the comrade who stood behind her. Gavin had that same damn look as before: pensive and intense, communicating through the void, his stare full of Daniel Craig secret assignments.

"Goodnight." Gavin kissed Audrey's cheek, gave her long, dirty-blonde hair three quick tugs, and left the room with a stunning, rather hippie-like smile floating in his blue-blue eyes. They *were* like the color of Van Gogh's starry sky. Dark and mysterious and as blue as the deep end of a Copenhagen ocean.

4

"Good morning," Gavin said as he opened the door of the dungeon before Audrey rang the bell to the service entrance, and the look she gave him asked him questions without her having to use words.

She invented ways around everything.

"I have cameras." He pointed to the corner of the doorframe. "I see all."

"You're here early."

"Every day."

She peeked inside. "You're alone?"

"Darcy doesn't usually come in until two or three."

"Bring me my keys," Kate yelled as the cab pulled away.

Gavin went toward the lot and gave Kate her keys, and once he returned, before Audrey knew what was happening, Kate was honking and blowing kisses out the window of her cherry-red Mustang as she took off down the street. A person might never know Kate winced with each shift of the gear stick, ached and throbbed around the curves and turns.

Because Kate took it like a pro.

Flinching was a reminder of why they'd made the hour trip

last night from Spring Hill to Tampa. They only had the week-end. Or Audrey did anyway, and she planned on making the best of it. It was only Sunday morning...

"What are you two up to?" Audrey asked with a raise of her brows. Kate had practically shoved her out of the cab, telling her to trust her own instincts and ring the buzzer beside the door. The girls hadn't talked much last night. They'd mostly slept.

"You didn't get the proper tour last night, and I was grumpy." Gavin ran a palm over the top of his head. He had light scruff there too.

"Grumpy, huh?" Audrey smiled, but maybe he was correct.

He had come off as a bit of an asshole. But every story had two sides, or three or four, and every-fucking-body had bad days. If torturing her clit and giving her the best orgasm of her life was *grumpy*, then she couldn't wait to see him elated.

Gavin was all business as he showed her a locker area, bath-rooms, and six hotel-sized rooms with codes and doors — two private, four with the infamous windows — and then he showed her the main floor. The communal areas. Last night, the open rooms had whizzed by in a flurry of bodies and groans.

He brought her into the first, where more than a dozen over-sized thrones lined the walls. Thirteen to be exact. Symbols were carved into the grain, on the heads and arms, emblems she couldn't make out but knew couldn't be arbitrary.

Two school desks were in the center. Those also appeared old and unique and were made of a dark wood. The tops were wide enough to hold a partial torso, leaving the head and neck, lower legs and feet, to spill over the edges — a perfect position to receive punishment.

Audrey felt a dull ache stab her pussy just picturing herself on one of the desks, naked and exposed and at her Master's mercy. But right now, Audrey longed to caress one of the crosses Gavin had guided her toward.

"Touch it," he said after he must've noticed her blurred gaze.

Her fingers inspected every inch — the binds, the smooth grain, the shape — her mind racing to catch the fantasy she'd rehearsed a million times while masturbating.

What would it feel like to be fastened to it? What would the man be like who did the binding? How would he hurt her, taunt her, own her? Would she go through with it?

"No one is here," he whispered, then touched the nape of her neck.

She shook from the friction, the nearness of his smell. Leather, cedar, shadows. He held his fingers there, not squeezing or pressing — only possessing.

Leaning into his touch, going with her instincts, she arched her back, closed her eyes, and breathed. His scent mixed with something else this morning. The polish on the cross. The smell of her own arousal.

He trailed his hand down her back, reached her tailbone, and took hold of her waist — not pressing, not squeezing — possessing her there too.

"How is your clit?" he whispered, and she didn't know why he was being quiet if the place was empty. But his tone and breath settled her, righted her, comforted her — made her forget she didn't know him at all, and yet she wanted his dick to jar her, wrestle with her, strangle her.

"Sore," she said, a sly smile on her lips as she shifted her gaze toward his.

In an instant, his hand was at her nape again, but now he did press and squeeze. He gripped her neck, twisting her face toward him, and then he kissed her.

This time, he didn't let her lead.

He gave her tongue, demanded her attention. He bit and sucked her lips to the point of bruising until neither of them could breathe and until their two bodies, fully clothed, became one.

Separating his swollen lips from hers, he paused, then smirked. "Do you want the *full* tour?"

"Are you clean?"

"I'm tested every few months. You?"

"Yes. Same."

Although she had no need to be tested every few months. She'd only had sex with Dell in the last fourteen years. Even after their separation, they'd fucked, but not since the divorce. The familiarity and need for a lover had replaced common sense once or twice ... or maybe a few times. But now, it had been over a year since she'd been breached, and she wanted nothing more than for Gavin to be the one to climb over her walls and lay siege.

"Take off your clothes," he said.

She found that she could do this. And would. Entering a dreamlike state, she undressed, wishing to please him even in this moment, wanting to present her body to him as a gift.

"I'll take care of you," Gavin said in a hush, his breath hitting her skin as he guided her to the cross. He buckled her wrists and ankles while continuing to reassure her. Audrey knew exactly what he meant by those words, and she was already drowning in them.

Once she was splayed out and naked in the formation of an X, Gavin ran his hands over every part of Audrey's body, tickling her into a further trance — the one his voice had started.

"Are you too sore to fuck?" he asked, but she could hear the darkness in his tone. He wanted to fuck her cunt while it was still sore. He was counting on it. He wanted to bruise what he'd hurt. Re-mark what he'd torn. Break the doll and glue her back together.

"No, Gavin. Please."

Reaching a hand between her legs, he pinched her clit without warning, and she screamed, then bit her lip and cursed. "Fuck..."

"You're not ready." She could still hear the darkness, the ache for her permission he desperately sought.

"Not ready for that, no. But you... I need you to..."

She heard the unbuckling of his pants and felt him draw near again.

"To what?" He stroked his cock along her seam. "You're so wet already, baby girl. You please me." His voice cracked just above a whisper, the ache apparent on the tip of his tongue.

Such a contradiction .... this man. His restraint and gentleness would soon be off the leash.

"Thank you, sir." Exhaling, she closed her eyes and waited, but nothing happened. He was a sadistic son of a bitch making her wait, playing these head games.

"I'm not afraid to give you what you need, Audrey. And we haven't set limits."

Did Gavin know what she needed?

Her mind began to race. Dell had known her for years, loved her, and he had been afraid to cross an invisible line they'd drawn in the sand. The trust they once shared had crumbled beneath heated arguments and second-guessing. Her need to submit was organic, and Dell's effort had not been.

But Dell probably wouldn't have been receptive to Audrey's desires even in the best of circumstances. Audrey had barely scratched the surface of her underlying fetishes when attempting to first explain to him how she'd recently begun to admit she liked pain.

Needed pain.

Wanted to be pushed.

Controlled.

Craved stinging and slapping.

Things she couldn't even imagine.

That her pussy ached thinking about being commanded and held and forced. That kink was more than an occasional nip or bite or pull of the hair.

"It's about taking care of me, Dell. Anticipating my—"

"I do that."

"Yes. I'm not saying—"

"You want me to hurt you to take care of you? Jesus, Audrey."

"We don't have to keep talking about it now."

"You should see a therapist."

"I'm talking to you. You're my partner."

"Sex partner. Life partner. This is something else."

"I know it's a lot to absorb in one night."

"I hold you down sometimes. Is that what you want? I'm not going to rape you."

"That's not what I said."

"I'm rough. We have it good, ABS. Don't mess with a good thing."

"Dell, I..."

Maybe she'd gone about it all wrong or used the wrong tone with him. Maybe if she'd opted for the boobs she knew he wanted, he might've been eager to try something new or forbidden. Or maybe he would've taken her to a place where they could've watched and learned.

And now here she was — watching and learning in a dungeon with a Dominant. A sadist. Someone who would strip away anything false and expose truth.

Audrey would be the best pupil under the best tutelage. It had only been two days of being in the presence of this man. Did Gavin know she would fall down and worship him? Beg for his cock? Beg for his ministrations? Beg to be beaten and used?

"How do you feel..." he asked, tapping her temple, "in here?"

"Aware," she said and paused. He seemed to be waiting for her to continue speaking. She swallowed. "Aware of my nudity.

Aware of each nerve ending. The cold on my skin. The empty space between my legs. The ache in my arms, legs, and hands."

He traipsed a finger from the top of her spine to the top of her tailbone. "What do you feel when I touch you?"

She blew out a breath and closed her eyes. "I feel alive. I feel fire." She believed this man could bring to fruition and then satiate the things she didn't even know she desired.

As she'd spoken, he'd taken items from the wall. One was a flogger, and he started with that. He teased her at first, swiping the leather ribbons across her backside, explaining that he was warming the skin, and then he struck her, but it didn't hurt. The material made contact with her back and ass many, many times, but it didn't hurt. It lulled her into that place between dreaming and sleep.

"What's your word?"

"King."

"I trust you'll use it with me anytime you need to. Yes?"

"Yes."

"The cane is a beautiful pain," he said, trading the flogger for it, rolling it around in his palm.

"Have you been caned?" she asked, craning her neck to try to see his expression.

"Yes," he replied without explanation. She could only see him out the corner of her eye. "A Dominant, especially a sadist, should always understand what it is he inflicts on others."

"But have you submitted?"

"I have." He touched the cane to her back.

It was cool and firm, reminding her of bamboo. Its power was deceptive.

"Who?" she asked, but then he struck her, and the blunt force on her buttocks took the breath from her lungs.

"Count to six, Audrey. Give in to me."

He struck her right thigh.

"One. Who?"

He struck her left thigh.

"Two. Who?"

He struck her across the ass again, and she screamed and buckled. Tears began to fill her eyes.

"Three."

"What's your word?"

"King."

"I'll push you far, Audrey. *Do you understand*?"

She nodded.

"Fucking say it."

"Y-yes. Yes, I understand."

"I trust you. Do you need to use your word?"

"Please. No. Don't stop, sir." She sobbed out the words in broken syllables. "I promise."

The cane made contact, and she let out another yelp of self-discovery.

"Count, Audrey." Gavin's breath was ragged. His voice like ominous clouds blowing across the sky.

"Four."

Five and six came in quick succession, landing across both butt cheeks, leaving a trail of fire over her body she wanted to still feel and absorb when she lay in her bed alone tonight.

Without warning, he dropped the cane, grabbed her hips, and entered her dripping warmth in one hard, vicious thrust, causing her to cry out in sheer shock from the force of it. His cock attacked her cunt like a starved hunter fighting for survival. The searing on her thighs and ass made for one hell of a cocktail.

Sex and pain, lust and resurrection — with a twist. No longer separate. Always side by side.

"Aware now?" he growled, thrusting in time with each word.

Unable to answer, Audrey's pussy surprised her by exploding around his cock, milking him.

"Did I give you permission to come?" he hissed on his next powerful surge.

"No, sir." Her voice and limbs shook.

"I should stop fucking your sweet hole and punish you, but this will be enough — fucking you raw inside your sore little cunt."

He pinched her clit despite his earlier promise, and she closed her eyes and cried at the contact. Reveling in the tears, she gave in to them, tasted them, wanted more of them, offered them on an altar for him.

Her body screamed with pleasure, imagining the bruises and stripes he'd just inflicted, the vision already pushing her to the verge of coming again. He didn't need to fuck her hard and fast. He only needed to hold his cock to the wall of her womb so she could absorb him into every fucking part of her soul.

"Sir?" she asked on a sob, sucking in the tears, holding back the wave of the threatening orgasm. "Please?"

"No." He pumped her with a renewed violence. Slow, deliberate violence. She sobbed openly, loudly.

"Please?" she yelled.

"No!" he replied, fucking with so much intention, picking up speed, that surely his dick would pierce though her insides. "This fuck is for me. That is also your punishment."

The onslaught went on and on. Audrey's mind went blank. Her throat dry. Only sensations. Bliss. Grass saturated from a hard rain.

"You will say my name when I come inside you."

"Gavin," she whispered. "Gavin..."

"Tell me you'll hurt for me. Tell me you'll please me."

He hadn't stopped his exertion. He maintained the pressure and pace.

"I will please you, sir. I'll hurt for you, Gavin. *Please...* I hurt for you."

She felt his knees buckle, heard his breathing change. He bit her shoulder as he poured his seed into her body, then slumped against her backside.

Audrey glanced up. Darcy was in the room, near the doors, and she'd probably already locked eyes with Gavin sometime during the vicious lovemaking because she didn't look fazed. Darcy had probably seen the whole fucking scene.

"Go open up room six," Gavin said to Darcy.

He unbuckled Audrey and lifted her into his arms. She laid her head against his chest.

"Look at Darcy," he said as she began to pass.

Audrey reluctantly shifted her head.

"There's nothing to hide from here." He lowered his mouth to her ear, and whispered, "Soon I'll have you in a room full of hungry people standing on the outside. And they won't be hungry for food, baby girl. They'll want you, your cunt. They'll look at you like you're the last meal on the face of the earth."

She buried her head in his chest.

"Look at Darcy," he repeated.

As Audrey met her eyes, Darcy nodded in agreement and understanding.

In awareness.

And then they followed her to room six. Audrey didn't even know if she'd seen room six before. During the tour, they'd all started to look the same.

Gavin laid her on the bed, said things to Darcy Audrey couldn't hear, and then he left the room. Audrey couldn't move. The pain was isolated but radiated. Everything ached and stung. And her chest felt hollow. She wanted the aftercare from *him*.

The warm washcloth touched her skin first, then Darcy's

fingers. She consoled Audrey with creams and oils and whispers. Then Darcy fed her pain medicine and water.

Afterward, Audrey finally managed to mumble, "Why didn't
he? Why isn't he...?"

"He..." Darcy began and stood, chewing on a fake fingernail
— orange to match her new highlights. "He hasn't topped
anyone for months, kid."

Darcy covered Audrey with a blanket. "You need to sleep."
She brushed her orange acrylic across Audrey's forehead,
closing her eyelids.

"Why?" Audrey croaked as Darcy reached the door, too
sleepy and flying too high to consider her mixed bag of
emotions.

"Same reason he won't do the aftercare, pet. He sets rules for
everyone else but breaks them for himself."

5

When Audrey awoke, Gavin stood in the white room, leaning against the wall with his damn biceps threatening to break through his motherfucking T-shirt.

She could live on those arms. Forage there.

"I'm here every day," he said as their eyes met in some kind of brutal understanding — the way they had from the moment she'd first made connection with his perfect Copenhagen blue.

"You told me."

"I own the place, Audrey. It's mine. I write a blog. I teach classes. Do meet-ups. This is my life."

"I needed you," she said as her voice cracked. The high was starting to fade. Her logic took over instinct.

"I'm here now," he exhaled the words, blowing out the regret and whatever else he held inside — the reasons for not topping anyone in months when he clearly needed a sub. And he ran the club? Owned it? Kate hadn't been joking.

"Who are you?" he asked, rubbing a thumb across her cheek.

"What? You want to know my last name?"

"I want to know *everything*," he said, but then his phone rang, and his eyes went blank, or they held so much emotion he didn't know where to put it. "I ... I have to take this."

Audrey couldn't help but glance at the screen, then he swiped the glass, said hello, and left the room.

The blanket draped across her naked body suddenly felt heavy even though her feet and hands felt cold. Her clothes must've still been on the floor by the cross. And that was also probably where she'd left her phone...

Audrey: I'm ready to go.

She fired off the text to Kate from where she now stood in the main room, slipping her shirt over her bra.

Kate: Already?

Audrey: I have stuff to take care of, and Gavin got an important phone call.

She finished dressing and shot off another text, one that might've been inappropriate.

Audrey: I saw the name on his screen. Michael??

Kate: I'll be there in like twenty.

"Hey, kid. You're up," Darcy said the moment Audrey entered the bar area. Her laptop was open on the counter, and her brows had been pinched in concentration as she stared at its screen.

"Yeah." Audrey shoved several strands of rather tangled hair behind her ear.

"Listen ... I hope you're not embarrassed about what I saw."

"What did you see?"

"I've seen *plenty* working here."

"I'm sure you have." Audrey took a seat on a stool. "Do you play?"

"Not here. Not anymore. It gets messy."

Audrey laughed.

"You have a dirty mind." Darcy tapped a fingernail to the tip of Audrey's nose.

"Isn't that a requirement? One of the 'rules'?" Audrey teased.

"You hungry?"

Audrey placed a palm over her stomach, chewed on her bottom lip, and looked into the distance.

Darcy closed the lid on the laptop. "Did I say something wrong?"

"He..." Audrey met Darcy's violet eyes. They were rare and deep and concerned. "Gavin got a phone call ... and he seemed—"

"You want advice?"

"You mean from, like, a bartender?" Audrey smiled.

"From someone who's known the guy too long." Darcy put her elbows on the granite and leaned closer. "Don't ask Gavin questions you don't want the answers to." She stared into Audrey's eyes, seeming to want to make sure she received the message, then she stood tall again. "*That* should be at the very top of his list of rules."

"What should be, Darc?" Gavin scowled.

"I think your pet is hungry."

"Kate will be here any minute," she began as Gavin and Darcy's eyes met, then parted. "I'm okay. I'll pick something up."

"Come, Audrey," he said as he walked off, his shoulders squared, seeming confident she would follow.

He led her to a kitchen. It was commercial but small. Whatever was cooking smelled delicious. He grabbed a bowl and ladled thick, creamy soup into it.

"I can take care of myself. I can feed myself, Gavin."

He lifted her onto the stainless-steel countertop, placed his hands on her thighs, and peered into her eyes. "Do you?"

This was one of those times when his stare nearly blinded her — the blue so bottomless and dark, penetrating anything in sight.

He took a breath, then spread her knees. Everything was

slow and deliberate. Thought-out. Planned. He stared at her center, at the material of her clothing, at how he moved his hands, his thumbs. Then he slid the bowl closer and dipped the wooden spoon into it, scooping what looked and smelled like chunks of potatoes and tiny pieces of bacon.

As he gently placed the warm concoction in her waiting mouth, she relaxed into his servitude, then fanned a hand in front of her lips.

"Too hot still?"

She swallowed the rest down. "It's really good."

A devious smile lit his eyes, crinkling the edges of his lids. "You always seem to have cream here." He wiped the corners of her lips.

"Gavin..."

"Say, 'Thank you, sir, for feeding me.'"

"Thank you, sir." Her mouth went dry as she waited for his next move. His blue eyes combed her brown ones for an eternity.

"Good girl," he finally replied, his voice sounding hoarse with need.

They were quiet as he fed her the remainder, using the same wooden spoon he must've stirred the pot with. The comfortable silence made each shift of their bodies and slurp off the utensil — each breath from their lungs — seem like its own entity.

She'd never been cared for like this. Well, as a child of course. But the memory wasn't there. And this one would never leave her.

Her phone chirped as he washed the dish in the sink.

"Kitten?" he called out over the faucet.

"Yeah. Where did she get that name?"

"She earned it." He dried his hands and smiled. "She purrs."

Audrey smirked as she hopped off the countertop and went

toward the door. But then she paused and glanced back at him — first tripping over the outline of his biceps but eventually finding his face again.

"I'm not sure when or if..." She blushed.

Gavin took a few steps, and now they stood about a foot or so apart. He folded his fucking godly arms across his broad chest. Audrey's mouth started to water. He didn't speak for a moment. He only stared intently at her heated face, her mussed hair, her sleepy eyes.

"We play, Audrey." His voice sounded cold, calculated. His eyes looked the same. She was beginning to learn she might never know what was a scene and what was reality. "This isn't a date."

"I know. I ... I'm sorry."

"Never apologize for saying what you feel."

"Yes, sir," Audrey breathed out on an exhale, sounding as if she'd just released long-suppressed beliefs.

His expression changed. His cold eyes looked warm and unfathomable even though she knew he tried to remain stoic. When she acquiesced to him, he had shifted though. And he should've been used to people obeying his commands, falling at his feet. Audrey couldn't figure out why he was so affected by a thirty-five-year-old woman who had no experience with his level of kink.

And, no, it wasn't a date.

Because she'd never felt this strong of a connection with a man at a restaurant while trying to get to know him while also trying not to seem too eager to have sex.

Everything in life was a game. There were just many different kinds. This sport with Gavin seemed easier. The rules were already set out.

He made demands.

She obeyed.

They played.

She could get what she needed, what she'd craved for years, and he would have his desires satisfied as well.

It was perfect.

Bodhi might very well live up to its name.

6

"Shut the fridge, Bryson."

"I don't know what I want."

"Well, figure it out with the door closed."

Audrey swept past him and shut it on her way to the toaster, where she grabbed the bread, then buttered it.

"Stop riding that thing in the house, Ricki," Bryson shouted.

"Don't call me Ricki," the younger boy said as he rode his skateboard to a halt in the middle of the kitchen. Rick was nine, and Bryson was twelve going on eighteen. The perfect gap, she'd thought, but it seemed now all they did was fight.

"Mom, tell him to stop riding it."

Audrey put the toast on the plate by each egg, shut the fridge door again with her foot, and shushed them on her way to the table.

"We'll be late. Come eat," she said.

"I want cereal."

"Rick ... come to the table."

He did, skateboard in hand, a scowl on his face, sitting down in a huff, a *humph* falling from his lips

"Where's your homework?" she asked.

"I want cereal."

"Too bad. I want a maid and a cook." She stood, scanning the room for any remnants of math pages. "Bryson, you have yours?"

"Yeah, in my backpack," he replied, scraping the last bit of egg and toast into his mouth. Slipping the bag over his shoulder, he took his plate to the kitchen, managing to kiss her cheek on the way.

"Love you, baby." She eyed him as he made his way to the front door. "Grandpa is staying this weekend. He'll be here when you get home."

"Again...?" Rick moaned.

"Eat," she demanded, eyeing Rick's plate.

"Yeah, whatever," Bryson grumbled, hand on the doorknob.

"Hey!" she yelled after him.

"What?" he sneered.

She'd let that go. Her guilt would let his attitude go.

She'd only gone to Bodhi two more times since the observation night. Twice. But kids always magnified any *supposed* parental misstep under a microscope to gain what they thought was leverage.

And besides, Audrey had intended to visit only during the weekends Dell had the boys, but the pull to be humiliated and abused was only getting stronger. Now she was asking her dad to stay so she could go more often. In just a few short weeks, she'd felt herself slowly slipping from this life and gravitating toward a new one. And she felt powerless to stop it.

"I love you, baby."

"I love you too," Bryson said on a sigh and then walked out the door.

She ruffled Rick's hair and stood.

"Where's your breakfast, Mommy?"

Sweet little Ricki. He noticed things no one else did. He

needn't have worried. She would run through the drive-thru after she dropped him at school, shove disgusting, greasy food into her mouth, and then stand on her feet all day and count other people's teeth. It would only be a few hours until she could kneel at *his* feet. Hours until she might be shared and then broken ... until she could scrub off the mask of civil obedience and walk into the kingdom of civil disobedience. It was a beautiful order. Submission made everything right. It gave her peace amidst chaos. Helped her not be afraid of what she couldn't control.

"Mommy..."

"Hmmm?" Audrey said and then held up a piece of paper. "What's this, baby?" She'd managed to read a few lines while daydreaming.

"I wrote it," Rick replied. "Why don't we have a Bible? Why do you send me to Catholic school when we don't have a Bible?"

"I can tell you wrote this," Audrey said with pride and a pat on her son's wrist. "And we do have one," she continued, although she wasn't sure.

She proceeded to silently read the essay her nine-year-old son had written about a woman who'd bled. A woman who'd been in constant pain for twelve years. Physicians had failed to stop it. This woman had dared to touch the Lord — because the Law stipulated people who bled should remain quarantined — in a crowd of people. And she'd only touched the edge of his cloak, an extension of him, a place where his energy still traveled — and her bleeding ceased in an instant.

The tale sounded familiar — a Sunday-school story she'd perhaps heard.

The word *blood* grabbed her attention. The need and desire the woman had to be clean and no longer suffer riveted her. The love Christ showed her, the honor he assigned her, all had Audrey fighting tears of empathy.

"Women were demeaned back then," Rick said.

Audrey gathered her wits. "Demeaned, huh?"

"Yeah, not treated right."

"What do you think is *right*, Ricki?"

"Mom..."

"Sorry, baby. *Rick...*"

"You know, they couldn't speak out or have a say. It took courage for the woman to be in that crowd when she wasn't even supposed to be around."

"She should've been ashamed of her blood?"

He shrugged. "Something, yeah. How do you think he knew the power went out of him?"

"What?"

"The scripture says the crowd was pressing all around him but that he knew who'd touched him. Jesus felt the power go out of him."

Audrey smiled, eyes blurring because of the damn tears. "Imagine Jesus is Superman. Imagine the touch of the woman was like a green finger of kryptonite."

Rick's eyes became as wide as shields.

Audrey nodded. "We're all energy, Ricki. Bits of matter. Jesus had to give up some of his own power to a woman, and he could feel it leave him. It was something so strong leaving his body and transferring to hers that he knew it in his bones, just the way Superman would know if kryptonite touched him."

Audrey paused and gazed at her son. One day, he would become a man and need to find his way in this crazy, beautiful world. "He gave of his energy ... and it healed her."

"Why are you crying, Mommy?" Rick tilted his head, looking both puzzled and fascinated. "It's just a story."

She cupped his chin. "Nothing is *just* a story, baby. This is *all* life."

All we had. All we were given.

She didn't know if she believed in an afterlife. But she wanted to. Maybe that was why she'd sent both boys to Catholic school. If her children had hope, then perhaps their faith alone might be enough to carry her doubts, and then she could live with them on the other side of the rainbow ... forever.

7

"No," she said, or had she only mouthed the word? At this point, she didn't know. But she was certain she felt her lips move.

He'd tortured her for what felt like hours — her body upright and chest facing the X of the cross, arms and legs beginning to go numb. She couldn't feel her hands or feet. And still, he played, seeming to desire bringing her to a new brink.

"No," she repeated this time aloud.

"No?"

"No, sir."

He continued to press two fingers into her tight hole. He fingered it, seeming not to worry about her comfort — which she thought was a royal mindfuck — and then he inserted a third digit after he unzipped his pants. Stretching her open, he finished whatever the butt plug he'd inserted and since removed may have failed to accomplish.

"No," she whispered, tears falling down her cheeks.

Gripping her dirty-blonde locks until her forehead faced the dark ceiling, he pumped his fingers inside her tight ring of muscle. Audrey was aware enough to realize Gavin knew she liked the pain despite her protests and tears. It hadn't been the first time he'd shoved his fingers inside that hole, but the minute the tip of his dick touched her there, she froze ... then glanced around the room — something he'd already taught her *not* to do. Every fucking eye was on her — her hole, her face, her tears.

"It's only us. Feel me." He slid in, probably only an inch, and she felt like she tore.

"No," she pleaded.

He'd often reserved touching her there during the throes of passion or right before or after an orgasm. They'd barely discussed anal — other than her saying she'd never been able to take a man that way. Gavin would ask her questions. Audrey made polite replies. Today had been the first time he'd asked her to wear a plug.

"Fuck ... you're still so tight."

"No," she cried.

Each no, although hushed and not meant for the audience, became more frantic. Her face hurt from crying and pleading in the same way it could ache from rolls of laughter.

"'No' what?" he asked through gritted teeth.

"No, sir," she said under her breath. "Not here. Please. Not here."

Nothing about this scene was refined, yet it had grace. She knew what that did to him. She wanted to please him.

"Yes, *here*," he said, inching his way into her ass slower than he had ever entered her cunt.

But still the movement, the centimeters he gained, felt like miles. It was difficult to control her reactions and her breath. She could only choke out her faux refusal, her awkwardness, as he pressed his chest to her naked back.

"Here," he hissed, his words oblivious to the entire room. "I will take your virgin little asshole. I own you here, and I'll fuck you any way I please. *Stop* being afraid of the pain and trust me to take care of you."

Each word caressed her ear and soul, sounding like lyrics to a favorite song — a quiet melody no one but the two of them could hear. Audrey and Gavin were the stars of a show.

And she knew he needed the show.

He needed to have this ultimate humiliation followed by redemption displayed for all to see. She wouldn't deny him. This was what she wanted as well: to be pushed outside her comfort zone. She wanted to tear down every wall she'd ever erected. Strike them with a wrecking ball.

Still, the tears flowed.

The sobbing coursed through her entire body. She could feel the emotion in her pussy, her veins, through her legs, like the first taste of a strong shot of alcohol.

And then it became a high.

And she would ride it all the way to the end.

She *would* bleed for him.

"Push back into me, Audrey." He moved slowly, gaining more centimeters. "Squeeze me. Milk me. Good girl. Now open your mouth for me," he said, then put a thin wooden paddle in it — his favorite, the one he'd thoroughly beaten her with prior to fingering her asshole.

"Bite this and bear down."

She obeyed as he filled her with about as much girth as she thought she could take. She hoped it was all of him. She wanted to please him. Her body gave way, sagging, but he held her hips, and the binds kept her weight. He wasn't thrusting ... not yet.

She cried, whimpered, wished to cover her nudity, and then she relaxed into the vulnerability — the purity of the moment.

She was clean.

Gavin was inside the dirtiest of places, and she was clean.

Free.

She had no shame.

Nothing to hide.

She bucked against him and sniffled. Stopped crying.

As he began to reach around and rub her clit, she heard him release a fantastic sigh.

"Hurt for me, baby girl," he whispered. As he massaged her into a frenzy, she bucked against him again and again. "Hurt for me."

"Mmm..." She nodded, and he removed the paddle from her mouth. "Please."

"Ask me to fuck you."

"Fuck me, sir. Fuck my ass. Please. I'm yours."

The beast within him charged, raged. The buckles about her wrists and ankles rattled, her skin slapping the wood as he fucked the virginity from her tight hole, as he spread her cheeks open and whispered to her over and over...

"You're beautiful. You're the one. Your ass is mine. Your holes are so beautiful. Mine to fill. To share. Mine..."

She could hear the tears in his eyes, feel them against her skin.

"I wish you could see what I see. I wish you could feel how tight you are around me. I want you to know the power you have over me."

And with those final words of truth, meant only for her and heard only by her, he became quiet. His chest shook against her backside as he nailed her to that cross and sacrificed her virginity to God and the room.

And as he came inside her, filling her with his warmth, she only came ... down.

After releasing her from the cuffs, he picked her up and held her in his arms, the same way he had the first time he'd bound her to the very same cross. Except now, his seed spilled from her asshole. Now ... every part of her body belonged to every part of him.

Nothing was hidden.

Eyelids heavy, limbs numb, she couldn't speak or even sigh. He carried her somewhere — her eyes closing and opening, her mind too drugged to see — through doors, past items and things, into a bathroom where he showed her specks of fresh blood on the tips of his fingers. He spread her open and licked it from her hole, cleaned her with his tongue, and then he bathed her, caring for her the way a parent does a small child.

All the while, she remained silent, limbs shaking, a baby girl in his charge. And until the trauma and shock — the subspace? — had passed, she wouldn't speak.

She'd only submit.

She knew she would do anything he asked.

Suck another. Fuck another. Play with herself in front of whomever he chose. Have her asshole torn open for show. She'd become what she'd dreamed of not so long ago...

A diamond shining through mud. Sunlight breaking over the horizon.

There was no going back now.

She'd stepped into the shadows to find the light.

8

Audrey blinked.

There were no windows in this room, and not having the sun to provide assistance as to the time was disconcerting. But there were many other things in here: pictures and books, items which told her this place was lived in and not just decorated — objects that made it feel like home and not a hotel suite.

Did Gavin live here in this tiny, windowless, homey space?

She heard water running. Light shone from underneath a door. God, she was sore. Gavin had cared for her last night. Or was it still tonight? Where the fuck was her phone? He'd bathed and oiled and massaged her. He'd spent a long time kissing her as she soaked in bubbles. The man could kiss as well as he could beat and burn and fuck. Maybe even better.

He was a little bit of everything.

But then he wasn't either, was he?

They weren't exactly dating. They'd covered that. He was here. And she was somewhere else ... on the outside. There was danger in this kind of thinking. She would ignore the consequences of what might come from overthinking or from not thinking things through at all ... and instead follow instinct.

Right now, she followed light.

Stepping out of the king-sized bed, she made her way naked and bruised and deliciously sore — her asshole reminding her what had been taken from her and what had been given to her — to the bathroom, where she gently pushed open the door.

Gavin stood over the sink, wearing his traditional jeans and a short-sleeved tee. But he was barefoot, holding a razor, and he had a gleam in his starry eyes — a luminosity that seemed custom-made for her.

"Do you know the story of Hannah?" Gavin's eyes remained fixed to Audrey's gaze.

Sometimes his stare, the way he wielded and honed it, made her feel more than naked.

She swallowed. "Who's Hannah?"

"You reminded me of a scripture earlier tonight." He applied shaving cream to his scalp.

So, it was still evening. Her days and nights were getting mixed up and crossed. Darkness and light.

"This is your room? I mean, you sleep here too?"

"Come here, Audrey."

She stepped inside the modest bathroom. It was warm and still a little steamy, and it smelled like the shower and whatever Gavin used for shampoo.

"Closer, baby girl. I want you to shave me."

"What?" She shook her head and felt her cheeks heat. "I can't. I might cut you."

He pressed his palms against the countertop, dropped his chin, and stared at the sink full of water. "You've already sheared me." He looked up, peered into her eyes, and placed the razor in her hand. "I trust you ... and I will guide you. It's not difficult."

Her eyes closed, then opened. Everything with him some-times felt like slo-mo. His arms were so close, threatening to tear his shirt to shreds with a sudden movement. His leather and cedar permeated her nose. Her flesh broke out in goose pimples as her nipples turned to stone.

"Concentrate. You'll shave me, and I'll tell you a story. Start with the sides. Top to bottom. Go ahead."

"Gavin," she whispered with a smile.

Taking her hand, he placed it where he wanted her to begin. "Care for me as you do yourself."

Their eyes met and locked for several heartbeats, seconds in which she couldn't breathe properly. Caring for herself had become something she did last, not foremost. He could surely see things in her gaze: hesitation and insecurities. He'd seen them the day he'd fed her the potato soup.

"Top to bottom." He dragged her palm with his toward his ear. "Good girl."

Her hand seemed to trip on the compliment, and he caught it and smiled. "I trust you, Audrey. Now listen to me.

"Hannah was a woman who hadn't a single child. And she desperately wanted one."

"I don't know why." Audrey smiled and shook the razor out in the sink full of hot water.

"Her husband's other wife had them, and she ridiculed Hannah for being barren. She wanted a child so much she took to praying in the house of the Lord. And one day, Eli the priest observed her and thought she was drunk."

"Why?"

"Because sometimes we believe what we see or what we think we see, Audrey. Not what's true. Now finish me, and I'll finish too."

His next words, though, sounded like a recital direct from the Bible.

"Hannah was praying in her heart, and her lips were moving but her voice was not heard. Eli thought she was drunk and said to her, 'How long are you going to stay drunk? Put away your wine.'

"'Not so, my lord,' Hannah replied, 'I am a woman who is deeply troubled. I have not been drinking wine or beer; I was pouring out my soul to the LORD. Do not take your servant for a wicked woman; I have been praying here out of my great anguish and grief.'"

The task complete, Audrey placed the razor next to the sink while Gavin's eyes combed her skin, crawling around, trying to get in. But she wouldn't look at him or let him go any deeper.

"What do you think those people saw earlier when you said no? When you begged me to stop? What if an outsider had witnessed our scene? What would they have thought? Many of us here know what it feels like to be considered 'wicked.'"

"Sir..."

"Your lips moved earlier tonight, baby girl." He ran the pad of his thumb along them, then he planted several kisses on her cheeks, forehead, and jawline. "Without sound. Were you praying to God for relief? Does anyone else know the words *in your heart*?"

"Gavin..." Her eyes started to water. "I don't pray." She glanced away, and he wiped her tears before they fell.

"Every time you come to me, it's an act of faith. God answered Hannah's prayer, and she said she was given a child 'because I asked the LORD for him.' No one else knows what's inside you *but you and Him*."

"You know what's in me." Her throat felt raw, and her stomach ached. "You see me."

"Come on, baby girl. You've had enough for one night. Let's get you back to Kitty Kate."

9

"Flowers," Dr. Marsha said, fingering the petals of the red tulips. "Who are these from?"

In the corner of the reception area near the filing cabinet, Audrey stood flicking through the manila envelopes in the drawer, trying to ignore the nasally and nosy (how ironic) voice of Dr. Marsha Cassopolis.

Dr. Marsha — because no one wanted to pronounce her last name, not even Marsha — was perfect. Her jet-black hair was curled and sprayed in the style of a movie star from the forties. Her clothes were like that too. Pencil skirts, blouses. Katharine Hepburn pant suits. Nothing out of place. She looked like she never ate or fucked or shat. A catalogue on the move.

Audrey tried to ignore the dentist's elegance and her nosy and nasally question, but when Diana had announced that she, Audrey — plain Jane Audrey Bianca Simone — was the recipient of two dozen tulips for the second time in six months ... well, Audrey wasn't sure Ms. Perfectly Groomed and Coifed could stand it.

"Those are Audrey's," Diana replied.

"Who are they from?"

"Mr. Stevens is in room three, Doctor," Diana interjected, "and Stephanie is on hold. Says she has an emergency."

After clearing her throat, the doctor went to her office, presumably to take the call from her daughter, Stephanie. Audrey mouthed a very grateful thank you to Diana the minute Dr. Marsha's pencil skirt swooshed from the room.

"Again?" Diana sighed with a roll of her eyes.

Audrey shrugged.

"Honey, he could send me flowers anytime."

What Diana failed to realize was Dell sent flowers because it was *all he could do*. He hadn't known what Audrey actually needed during their marriage, never cared. He didn't even remember flowers made her sneeze. Didn't remember she hated dill pickles but loved sweet ones. Didn't always remember to buy a card on her birthday or care to understand why she sometimes wanted a vacation — alone (although she'd never taken one).

No, he did flowers because flowers were easy. A man could buy them, present them like an offering, and then go to bed feeling good about himself while never really knowing what made a woman tick.

Besides, flowers lived only days, then died.

And they weren't even her favorite color.

It didn't matter.

"I'm trying, ABS," Dell used to say. *Trying* meant taking her to *his* favorite restaurant, holding her wrists above her head while he fucked her for all of sixty seconds. Trying meant never asking the kids to brush their teeth or go to bed.

The flowers were only a reminder of the failure.

Hers and his.

Too bad he'd never understand that.

Maybe he needed a woman like Diana. A woman who seemed content with mediocre. A woman whose fantasies weren't sick. Dell thought he was still in love with Audrey. That was why he sent flowers. But he loved a dream, and that dream had died soon after Rick had been born. Counseling, alcohol, nights on the town, communication, ideas — none of it had saved them or their marriage.

Audrey had to save herself.

She made her own misery now. Her own happiness. Every decision — *hers*. And that was why she'd decided to go to the dungeon. Because it was her choice, and because stepping outside society's definition of "normal" gave her greater freedoms than several years of marriage had ever dared to achieve.

10

"Did you get my arrangement?"

The crack of the little league bat distracted Audrey from Dell's question. Rising, she cheered along with the other thirty or so parents at the field watching their children play, and then she took a seat on the bench next to him again. It was a warm Monday afternoon in September. The fading sun still blanketed the field.

"Did you get the—?"

"Yes, I'm sorry. I did. Thank you." Audrey kept her gaze trained on the field, never making eye contact with Dell. The hurt in his eyes was more than she could bear.

"ABS..."

"Please. I don't want to—"

"Jesus, Audrey. They're just fucking flowers."

At first, she looked around to see if anyone was paying attention to his mouth, and then she finally met his cerulean eyes. The crinkles around the edges hurt almost as much as his stare. The lines were one of his trademarks. Cuter than dimples.

"I want you to move on. See other people."

He pushed the soles of his sneakers across the concrete. "I see people."

Facing forward, both of them stoically kept their eyes on the balls and bats and caps.

"You fuck people," she said quietly after turning and putting her lips near his ear.

"Don't you?"

"I'm not doing this." Her attention snapped back to the inning. What fucking number were they on now?

"Right." He snickered. "You're not doing this."

He made that insidious noise again. Maybe his cute little Dell crinkles weren't so cute anymore.

"Isn't that why our marriage hit the fan? Because you can't talk to me ... or have a simple conversation without running from it?"

He'd been the runner. She'd tired of articulating her feelings to a man who lived by the motto of the French: *c'est la vie*. So, Audrey had eventually stopped initiating the act of "talking" — or fucking. Her ex called it running.

"This is what I don't have to do anymore. We don't need to have this conversation."

The crowd hollered. Audrey stood, clapped, then sat again. They watched Rick finish his game in tolerable silence. The parents roared, but Dell and Audrey whispered things telepathically.

We can't talk about the past.

I miss you.

You miss a wife.

I miss you.

She ignored his palpable need to have things right in his world — right meant winning back the affection of his wife, and then what? — even though the two of them together would be all wrong. Not a solution or an answer.

Body language did the speaking for them: arms taut at their sides, thighs rigid, fingers gripping the bench.

Several minutes later, people stood and whooped and clapped. Game over. Rick's team had won. As they eyed their son on the field, celebrating with his mates, Dell inadvertently placed his hand on the small of his ex-wife's back, causing her to flinch, then wince.

Gavin had painted quite a picture on the canvas of Audrey's skin the other night. The bruises from his fingers and palms and his favorite paddle were still fresh, tender.

But of course, Dell thought her flinch had been because of him. And maybe it was — a little. She didn't want to give him false hope or tease him. Because he seemed to think sending her flowers for forgotten anniversaries was enough to woo her back into his bed.

"Dad, do you want to get pizza with us?" Rick asked as he stepped into the backseat of the SUV.

"Not tonight, buddy," Dell replied as he flicked a heated stare at Audrey, the conversation from the stands apparently not over.

Audrey bent forward to tie her shoe while Dell gave his son a kiss, and then he closed the door. The engine was on. AC blasting. All the doors were closed. The former husband and wife stood on the outside of the tinted windows. Rick was probably already viewing something on his phone.

"This is what you wanted? Why you left me?"

"What are you talking about?" Squinting toward the window, she ascertained Ricki had his face buried in an app, his earbuds tucked into his canals.

"Wearing a hoodie in this fucking heat." Dell shook his head. Her face must've flushed a million shades darker than those stupid two dozen tulips Dell had sent to the office, though she pretended not to know what his snarky words implied.

How had he figured it out?

When she'd tied her shoelace...

The flinching earlier too. The pain, not disgust, that had been on her face.

"You want some douchebag to beat the shit out of you?" He reached for the hem of her sweater, but she swatted his hand away.

"I can't do this. Rick will see us fighting."

"I'm not raising my voice," he said, stepping a few feet from the vehicle. "Can I trust you anymore, Audrey?"

"What?"

"Maybe I should have full custody."

"You don't want that."

"I don't want this fucked-up shit."

"It's not your fucked-up shit. It's not fucked up—"

"What if our kids see this?" He reached for the hem again.

"I'm careful." She took two steps backward.

"I just saw it, ABS." He swept a palm over his face. "Christ."

"Please, Dell. I don't owe you an explanation. Please."

"I love you, Audrey."

Audrey worried he had said *that* too loud. Rick shouldn't hear this conversation. She had to resist the urge to plug her own ears. Her son's buds were looking pretty damn good right about now.

"You love an idea. The house. The fence. The dog. You love a picture on the wall."

"No." He stepped closer. "I miss you. Us."

"Dell ... I changed."

"I know. And I still want you."

And there was the downfall of their marriage in a nutshell. *Still* being his operative word. The vows *for better or for worse* meant he could continue to treat her like she had been afflicted with the *worse* — or a curse. It wasn't acceptance. And his next words proved it.

"You should be seeing someone about this, ABS."

Meeting him like an opponent in the ring, eyes fixated and narrowed, hands at her sides, fists balled, she said, "I am," with no room for error in her tone.

Minutes later, after Dell left and before she pulled out of the parking lot, Audrey shot off a message to Kate.

Audrey: Dell knows. He threatened me.

Fuck ... was the text a mistake?

The girls had spent a few nights in a hotel bed. They sometimes texted. But she'd never opened up much about her ex. Kate was her kinky friend, her accomplice in the world of fetish. Not her cry-on-my-shoulder-and-sleep-over-and-watch-a-movie friend. But Audrey didn't have many friends. One who had her own list of adult things to keep her busy: five kids, a mortgage, a job, and a disabled husband. Needless to say, they didn't talk much. Girls' night out had become less of a ritual and more of an annual thing you did to catch up and not be forgotten. The hairdresser knew more about Audrey's life than Kendall.

Too late. The message was out there now, in the ether.

Kate: Like physically? Where are you?

Audrey: No. With the kids. Rick just finished his baseball game. About to head home. About to burst into tears. It's a toss-up.

Kate: Text me your address. I'm bringing a bottle of wine. See you in about thirty or forty-five.

Audrey put the car in reverse. "We won't be getting pizza now, buddy. Mommy's friend is coming over."

Would texting Kate prove to be a mistake? Other than the fact that they'd already shared intimacies Audrey had never experienced with another human being on planet earth — not counting Gavin or Dell — what did they have in common?

Could what they'd shared be considered intimacies? Or only fantasies? Were they profound? Or only pornographic?

"Rick, did you hear me?" Audrey yelled, and he took out his buds.

Who put the labels on sex? Where did they come from? Would Dell really try to take the kids?

Repression: disallowing a desire to be expressed.

Suppression: conscious exclusion of feelings; discipline.

"We're going home for dinner."

Ten minutes to the house felt like an hour as the radio played right alongside the questions circling like birds of prey in her mind.

11

"God, it smells good in here."

Audrey was making the boys' favorite: fried chicken and macaroni and cheese. Bryson loved the chicken, Rick the mac n' cheese.

But which one had opened the front door? And had they asked who it was first?

"You can cook too, huh?" Kate asked, a huge smile on her face, the black spaghetti straps of her cotton camisole barely containing her triple-Z tits. The color of the tank and tiny, under-the-ribcage cardigan matched her straight, just-past-the-shoulder-length hair. It looked good on her. Everything did.

Audrey returned the smile while tending to the tasks at hand.

"You seem in good spirits now."

"Have to be," she said, nodding toward the kids. "And food will do that to me."

"You haven't eaten yet."

"Fine. Cooking clears my mind."

"And wine." Kate held up the bottle in perfect alignment with her billowing cleavage. The woman was a plush pinup, two times the size of Monroe. All curves and a squishy middle and an ass resembling large globes.

"Mom, we're gonna throw the football." Bryson entered the room, tossing the ball from hand to hand.

"You didn't meet Kate."

"I did," Rick yelled.

"I met Rick." Kate grinned. "But not you," she said, extending a hand to Bryson.

"Did you ask before you opened the door, Rick?"

"You told me your friend was—"

"Ricki, you have to ask." Both boys neared the slider as Audrey nagged. "It's almost dark. Dinner is about ready."

"Call us," Bryson said, face through the opening, and then he closed the glass.

"Wine opener?" Kate asked.

"Second drawer." Audrey nodded toward it, then she took out two glasses.

Kate poured. "Your kids are cute. The pictures you've shown me don't lie. You and your husband made some good-looking kids."

"Ex." Audrey exhaled the early evening's game and the unwanted conversation while staring at the coconut oil popping around the Rice Chex-plastered chicken.

"Mmm."

Warm hands on her shoulders startled Audrey — soft hands, small and firm — but then they put her at ease as Kate massaged her aching muscles.

"God. You're tense," Kate said from behind Audrey, her breath hitting her shoulder blades.

"Dell saw the bruises."

Kate's magical fingers ceased tending to Audrey's aches.

"Don't stop," Audrey groaned, rolling her head side to side.

Kate gathered Audrey's dirty-blonde hair and started to

braid it. Anytime someone played with Audrey's hair — something Dell had rarely done — it felt amazing. Soothing.

"Gavin likes to do this."

"What?"

"Braid my hair before we play."

"I can do it too." Kate put a band she grabbed from the counter at the end when she finished and then continued the massage. "Tell me what he said?"

Who? Audrey wasn't conscious of chicken or noodles. Scalp tingly and muscles screaming *thank you* had her in a stupor, and she hadn't touched the wine.

"Come on"—Kate slid her fingers down Audrey's back, then slapped her ass—"tell me what he said."

"Fuck you. My ass still hurts too."

"That's what your husband said?" Kate grinned.

Audrey put the lid on the chicken, turned it down, then took a large sip of wine. "He accused me of leaving our marriage so that I could get the shit beat out of me by a douchebag."

Kate grinned, appearing to fight a fit of laughter.

"It wasn't very funny at the time." Audrey cracked a smile.

"We own that, babe." Kate gulped wine. "That's why it's funny now. *We own this shit.* These bruises"—she pulled on her tank, exposing her multicolored tits and pink nipples—"belong to us. Not your husband."

"Mommmm..."

"Jesus Christ. Put yourself away."

Kate laughed. Audrey sighed, then swallowed more red wine.

"Bryson isn't being fair ... again."

"Wash your hands, Rick. You know what happ—"

"Mom, he changes the rules."

"I don't want to hear it. Wash your hands."

Bryson had come inside too, sweating and complaining. The

noodles were almost finished. A second glass of wine was poured. Several minutes later, hands clean, blessing said, the four of them ate together, made jokes, and smiled. They discussed sports, electronic games, and school.

Being around Kate was easy, intimate — a friendship that reassured her all was right with the world. To Audrey, it seemed like she'd known Kate for much longer than just a few months. It was silly to have been worried about texting her.

Dishes washed, boys in bed, and the two women still seemed to have a lot to talk about. They'd been slumped on the couch in the front part of the house in the dark for a while — Kate's head in Audrey's lap, her breasts splitting to the sides but pointing up, wine in her gaze and breath.

"When did you meet Peyton?" Audrey asked, head against the cushion. The room tilted a little.

"He didn't waste time asking me to be his submissive." Kate fingered the lariat style necklace with the double-heart pendant resting between her breasts. "Do you want to hear about the night he collared me?"

Audrey's breathing changed. Her eyes must've changed too because Kate took her silence and tells as signs to continue.

"The bastard wore shorts." Kate laughed. "It was just the three of us. But he wore his stupid swim trunks. Thank God Gavin forbids them at the dungeon, or I swear Peyton would never change out of them. And when we first entered the main chamber at Bodhi, I thought Gavin was going to shit himself when he saw Peyton wearing his surf shorts and flip-flops."

"And what did you wear?" Audrey paused, timing her joke perfectly. "Nothing?"

"You're being naughty." Kate squeezed Audrey's waist.

She laughed and buckled. "Stop."

"I wore a corset dress. It was black." She smirked. "It pushed my boobs way up and out." Kate cupped them, and Audrey had to fight the urge to stare at the swell.

"Gavin arranged the whole damn thing. He put two of the thrones front and center, facing each other. The other chairs had been set aside. The desks and crosses too. It was just the two chairs and two lines of candles creating a pathway to the make-shift altar." Kate became quiet. She fingered the pendant of the two intertwined hearts.

"We wanted it to just be the three of us. And we said a few words to each other, and Gav recited some of his fancy Bible things, and then Peyton put this on me." The hearts were clenched in Kate's fist. "I don't take it off. Ever. It's the only thing that never leaves me."

Kate sighed and closed her eyes while Audrey fixated on the rise and fall of Kate's chest, trying not to think of what it would be like to share such intimacies with Gavin ... or what thinking about being collared by him, at this point in their "relationship," meant.

"I saw Peyton for the first time at a meet-up." Her eyes opened, and the blue looked drunk on love not wine. "The connection was immediate, Audrey. It was one of those things, you know? We just clicked."

Audrey hadn't stopped staring into Kate's blue orbs of comfort and truth. "We click."

"We do." Kate's voice had never sounded more reassuring as she reached up and stroked Audrey's cheek.

Audrey leaned into the touch, smiled, and changed the subject — her mind suddenly on the intimacies she did share with Gavin already. "I told him about the kids." He'd found out about her boys on Audrey's second visit to Bodhi.

"Tell me." Kate's eyes grew wider than her tits.

"It's a night for stories, huh?"

"Yes. And a night for friendship and love."

Audrey swallowed, inhaled, and proceeded to regale Kate
with details...

"I didn't think you'd show again," Gavin had said to Audrey the
second weekend she'd visited as they stood outside one of the
observation windows.

A woman hung from the ceiling near the foot of the bed, red
jute rope fastened about her forearms and biceps and wrapped
beneath and above her chest, showing off her Master's art of
Kinbaku. Her nipples were being squeezed by clothespins. The
woman was stunning, her face a still frame of sublime content-
ment. A man, presumably her Master, stood behind her,
inserting an object Audrey couldn't quite make out into her
vagina.

"I thought I pushed you too far."

Gavin hadn't touched her yet tonight, but already his words
tugged at her heart. She'd told him how she longed to be
pushed. "Didn't Kate tell you anything?"

"I don't ask Kate for answers only you can provide." His voice
sounded so level while Audrey could literally feel her breath
growing more ragged by the second.

After a moment of what seemed like purposeful, meditative
silence — and Audrey could now decipher that the object in the
woman's cunt was a ruler the Dom had no doubt already used
on her ass — Gavin asked, "Why did you come back?"

Audrey turned her face toward him. The perfect amount of
scruff peppered his jaw and scalp — the right amount to cause a
burn, leave her thighs and cheeks stinging and pink. "I always
planned on coming back. It's only been—"

"Two weeks," he said and began to braid her hair.

He tugged at each cord harshly as he wound the sandy

strands together. And did he always have a rubber band in his pocket? Who knew what else he kept in there.

"What's your full name, baby girl?"

"Why? Do want to check up on me?"

He yanked on her braid until her eyes combed the ceiling, his grip and intense starry stare indicating yes.

"I checked up on you," she said while he trailed a finger from her chin to her chest. "I've read your blogs."

"Not all of them." He released his hold on her long, dirty-blonde hair, and they both fixated on the scene.

The woman was making sounds loud enough to pass through the walls. Incoherent grunts begging for release. But the man only removed the ruler and hit her with it while telling her what looked like: *Be a good girl. Hold still. Breathe with me.*

"No, not all of them."

"I mean, there are some no one has seen — or ever will." He lifted her skirt and slipped a hand inside her panties.

"Gavin..."

"Sellers," he said, a thumb on her clit.

She could feel his smile against her neck, heard it in his voice.

"Sellers..." But she knew that too, from his website. She smiled in return while trying to remain upright and fuck his hand. "It's Simone. Audrey Bianca Simone." She inhaled sharply as two fingers went into her aching heat. "I'm divorced."

"I remember ... and you're curious." He bit her earlobe. "And..." He bit her some more, each nibble getting deeper by the second. "You're so fucking beautiful..."

"I'm a mom," she said, and he stopped.

There.

Audrey had said it. And she wanted the words to lay stagnant in the air the way the humidity often did. She wanted him to taste them, digest them, think about what coming here meant to her.

"Please," she begged, but he removed his hand, letting her skirt fall. A moan passed her lips. "I can't come here whenever I feel like it." The back of her head rested against his neck. "And I feel a lot, Gavin." She paused. "Sir..."

Flipping her around, he pressed her spine to the window and stared into her eyes like he wanted to reside in them. "I'll never make you choose, Audrey." He paused, letting the words anchor to her soul. "How old?"

"Twelve. Nine. Both boys."

"My son is twenty-two. Ahhh. You don't look surprised. Kate told you."

Audrey nodded. Kate had told her a little about Michael on the ride home after her first weekend there — his age, where he lived — the day she'd seen the name flash on his phone screen.

"Michael and I don't see eye to—" Gavin stopped because someone exited the white room, interrupting them. The blinds went down too.

"I have to go to bed." Audrey yawned. "And I think my story is boring you." Or Kate knew other things about Michael, things Gavin had failed to say.

"No... I'm sleepy too."

Maybe the second bottle of wine had been a bad idea. Audrey's stomach and mind turned. "Stay here. I don't want you driving."

"Mmmkay," Kate said as Audrey stood.

Upon reaching the door to her room, Audrey stopped, turned, and smiled. "Come on. I'm not gonna make you sleep on the couch. Jeez."

It had been a long time since Audrey had shared the bed.

Well, Rick still liked to climb in from time to time. But this would be different. A grown-up. Someone she could rely on, lean on, talk to in private.

"Do you love him? Does he love you?" Audrey whispered as they lay in the bed, her back facing Kate's chest. A foot or so rested between them in the king-sized bed, covers at their waists.

"Yes."

"How does that work?"

"The same way it works for anybody."

"But he shares you."

"Yeah ... we share. It's what we both want." Kate paused, inhaled. "Falling in love doesn't happen often, Audrey. Not to me anyway. And connecting with someone ... well, God, it's like cosmic."

Kate's hand grazed Audrey's waist. Her breath tickled her nape.

"Turn around. Look at me," Kate said, and Audrey followed her edict. "I'm kind of ... pansexual. And maybe a little poly, although, like I said, I don't fall in love easily, but I play and fuck without following society's rules. Do you understand?"

"I'm trying to. I want..." How drunk did Audrey feel? Drunk enough to talk like this? Drunk enough not to giggle or have a bushel of roses color her cheeks. "I want him to push me." Fascinated by the rise and fall of Kate's chest, Audrey blinked.

"He will," Kate said with a strain as she slipped a strand of sandy hair from Audrey's lips.

The only sound heard was their breathing, shallow and hot, Audrey wearing a cotton T-shirt that read *Girls Rule*, and Kate in her fucking black cami without the bra, without the tiny cardigan, without her skirt. A black spaghetti-strap cami and her lack of inhibition the only things on display.

"Do you want my advice?"

"Have you ever not given it?" Audrey had learned that fact in the time they'd spent chatting and texting despite their avoidance of certain topics.

"Don't ask so many questions. Don't fight what's right. Only if it feels wrong. And not because of your *idea* of wrong. Trust your instincts like I told you. Because you've been conditioned to react a certain way."

"Some people like society's thumb. It comforts them."

"Not you."

"I'm afraid of consequence."

Kate smiled. "No, you're brave. Or you wouldn't even be lying here in this bed with me. You're afraid of life without risk too. Do you think your husband—?"

"Ex-husband."

"Yeah, him. Do you think he meant what he said about the kids?"

"No, but I know Dell will never see me the same way again. I don't know if I can talk to Gavin about this kind of stuff."

"Kids won't be the barrier. You know about Michael. You've told him about your boys. You don't need to be afraid of the pendulum of control. It swings every which way." Kate hesitated a moment as she stared at Audrey's lips. The women seemed to share a heartbeat. "You'll be the only thing standing in the way of moving forward with him."

Kate's pale-blue gaze grew more intense, but then she turned over. Audrey could feel how much Kate had wanted to kiss her. The restraint in her eyes and exhalations of her breath. And was it wrong that Audrey wanted to reach out and stroke Kate's back, graze her shoulder with her fingertips, plant a kiss on her neck?

Maybe the wine had gone to Audrey's head, or maybe she was truly entertaining what touching or kissing a woman might feel like. Throbbing in places only Gavin had recently awakened — was that why she wanted Kate to touch her? — Audrey rolled over as well and went to sleep.

Kate had left early, probably before the sun came up. She had a day job too, traveling to St. Pete to take care of marine animals. A bottle of ibuprofen and a note lay next to Audrey's phone.

Take two of these — or, fuck it, four — and call me in the morning.
Hey, and maybe the ex needs to never see you the same way again.
Gavin will see you differently too — through you and inside you.
There won't be a place left on you Gav won't exploit or explore.

PS - I had blue balls all fucking night.

Audrey smiled thinking of her pansexual/poly/kinky friend...

She'd been right telling Dell she'd changed. The welts he'd seen were only a visible manifestation of the writing on her heart — the story waiting to be penned, then read.

She would hide the colors of freedom from the innocents while playing with fire alongside the trailblazers.

12

Perfectly round nipples. That was what he'd said.

Funny she remembered the words of an old boyfriend now, sitting at a traffic light, after all these years. It was what he'd told her the first time he'd laid eyes on her naked body. Maybe she was pondering the age-old comment because Kate had just exposed her beautiful breasts in Audrey's kitchen the other night.

Perfectly.

Round.

Large.

Nipples.

Audrey had been only eighteen when he'd first told her that. Eighteen-year-old breasts were perfect no matter how unperfect their owner thought them to be.

And hers had been perfect.

Although she hadn't thought so at the time. Hindsight and all that bullshit.

She'd fed two babies with those perfectly round nipples. And long before that, given them to boys — peers — to suck and nip, and then offered them to men to bite. The one who'd called them perfect, though, he'd gotten away. A musician intent on fulfilling his dream of drumming for some hardcore rock band. And she'd refused to go with him to New York City. She'd stayed behind, slowly beginning her descent into buying into the dream of the white picket fence and 2.5 kids.

The last twelve years had flown by in a haste of diapers and pacifiers and tantrums and homework and theme parks and crying and giggles and bedtime snuggles. Twenty-three to thirty-five in the blink of an eye.

She'd married the first kind, sweet, funny man who showed interest. And he was kind and sweet and funny. Pretty interesting too. He liked science and mechanics, stars and gears.

He'd been safe.

He'd come home at night.

He'd remained faithful, loyal.

He'd changed diapers and the oil in the cars.

Some women might've wished to scratch Audrey's eyeballs out for daring to take such a man for granted. But the lonely she felt night after night said otherwise. It ate her alive. The companionship they'd shared at the outset had vanished, disappeared ... almost as though it had never been there.

Had she imagined it?

Audrey felt like she'd become a fixture — no different than a favorite bedside lamp or the fluffy thousand-thread-count sheet set. The mailman who came each day — every fucking day — whether there was rain, snow, or sleet, hurricanes, or acts of God. *The mailperson was there*. Did the home dweller care anymore who carried or sorted the mail? As long as it was just there...

This worked both ways.

Audrey knew she'd taken Dell for granted too. He'd become

a body in the bed to keep her warm, to placate the hollow between her legs, to make sure bills were paid, to discuss whose house would host Thanksgiving next. All the essentials. Intimacy took a backseat to arrangements and necessity. Staring into each other's eyes simply because one felt the soul resided there and the other needed to find it ... had been replaced by goddamn life.

No one had time for that bullshit. And it was bullshit, right?

Kissing ... a mere peck on the cheek, a way to say hello or goodbye. The tongue a device for licking genitals (occasionally), or discussing mundane stuff, or eating.

What year had they met? She had been in love with him. Had been.

"Mommy, the light turned green."

She tapped her fingernails across the steering wheel. "What, Rick?"

"The light, Mom," Bryson chimed in the moment a horn honked. "Jeez, you're a space case."

Catching the roll of Bryson's eyes in the rearview, Audrey put the weight of her foot on the pedal and went in the direction of the house where she'd spent the good years of her life — the one where she'd forgotten the definition of the word *home*.

Her boys' memories of these times would be the opposite ... she hoped. She'd have to work harder to be present, to not "space out."

It wouldn't be long now ... a few more days until the weekend ... until Bodhi. Three more days until she hit the road with Kate. Destination: the bed of a man — or the cross of a man — who owned her but hadn't claimed her, who understood her base needs and fulfilled them.

The boys would understand when they were older and became men themselves. Had their own proclivities.

It would all click.

Hormones and girls and responsibility. That stupid "Cat's in the Cradle" song chided her at three o' clock in the morning.

Bryson and Rick would forgive her absent mind because something had to satiate her unworthy heart.

13

"How about I push the cart?"

"No, he said I could."

"No, I didn't. He's lying."

"Aren't you guys too old to fight over who pushes the cart?"

That drew a scowl from Bryson and a loud no from Rick. But they continued to fight, and Audrey continued to play referee until she couldn't take the bickering anymore. She brought the shopping cart to a halt in the middle of aisle five — the cereal, the coffee, the carboard containers of milk.

Narrowing her eyes and smooshing her lips into a hard-pressed line, she whisper-growled, "Do you remember the story of Lightfoot and Quickfoot?"

"Not this again, Mom, please," Bryson pleaded. "You're embarrassing me."

"*I'm embarrassing you*?"

"That's my favorite story."

"Thank you, Rick."

Rick stuck out his tongue. Bryson threw an air punch at his little brother's face, which only caused Rick to stick out his tongue again.

Audrey beat her palms on the handlebar of the metal cart and hissed, "Stop it! What did the mother alligator tell her children?" She looked between her sons. Bryson looked handsome even with a scowl on his face, and Rick would be sure to try to one-up him any chance he had.

"She said," Rick began, with a shit-eating grin on his face and a know-it-all tone, "'no fighting. No biting.'"

Bryson folded his arms across his chest and narrowed his eyes.

"And she said she means it too! Do you understand, Bryson Christopher and Rick Denton?"

"Yes," they said in unison.

"I'm pushing the cart." She barreled toward the buy-one-get-one-free Cheerios.

"Hey, Mom, what's that on your wrist?" Bryson asked just as a man from school approached. The fucking Catholic school.

Audrey pulled the long sleeves past her wrists, cupped the sweater in her palms, and smiled at the man who had just said hello to all three of them as he passed. She gave Bry the death stare.

"Seriously, Mom," he whispered.

"I burnt it on the curling iron."

Bryson stared at her hair. Thankfully, Rick didn't seem to be paying them any mind. He was fixated on the boxes of sugary cereal lining the lower shelves, eyeing the prizes and cartoons.

"Your hair is already wavy."

"Yeah," she said, ruffling his mop of brown hair, "what do you know about women and hair?" She grinned. "Do you have someone at school you like?"

Audrey hoped she'd done a good job deflecting his concern. It was bad enough she had to be careful when joining the kids at the beach or the pool, but the burns would have to be more inconspicuous. Even though she was in the middle of the grocery store — the church-goer feet away, the kids and the shopping list, the mom things ... and the things and the things and the things — she still had to press her thighs together remembering how the hot wax felt as it dripped onto her arms and thighs, the fullness she felt when he thrust deep inside her body. The things he whispered as he burned her, the look in his eyes.

"Maybe..." Bryson said.

"Huh?"

"God, Mom, are you even listening?" Bryson rolled his eyes. "You ask me a question, and then you ignore me. You don't ever listen anymore."

"That's not true," she said, then turned to Rick. "Get off the floor, Rick. Come on."

"I want these. Please, please, please," Rick whined. "The box says I could win—"

"I don't care. No."

"See..." Bry said, full of his twelve-year-old ego, "not listening."

Audrey grinned and play-punched his bicep. "Yeah, yeah, yeah," she joked. "Come on, I'm starving, and then I have to get you home. Grandpa will be there soon."

"Are you leaving again?"

Her stomach dropped. "What do you mean?"

"With Kate." Bryson looked serious — more serious than a kid should ever be. "Mom, is she, like, you know..."—he dropped his voice—"your girlfriend?"

Audrey eyeballed him, wondering if he could read the infatuation in her eyes. "No." She pushed the cart, wheeling it toward the prepackaged meats. "Do you guys want hotdogs?"

"Yeah! Let me pick," Rick said, bouncing and running his hands across the plastic packages.

"I've seen her with you," Bryson said.

Audrey set some other meats into the cart and sighed. "Adult relationships are complicated, Bry."

"I'm not a baby. That's what you say about you and Dad too. I'm not a baby."

"Fine, fine, fine." She blew hair from her eyes. "Kate and I are friends. Kate is … God, Bryson, you're too young."

"She likes girls?"

"She likes both, Bry. Men and women." His eyes widened. He stared at shelves of meat. "She doesn't have rules about these things the way other people might. And it's okay. She doesn't—"

"God, Mom, do we have to have this conversation in the middle of the grocery store?"

"You asked, bud."

"Yeah," he laughed, "because I thought you were a lesbo."

"What?" Rick asked, putting his favorite green-and-white package of bun-length hot dogs in the cart. "Who is a lesbo? What's a lesbo?"

"Shhh," Audrey said. "No one, Rick."

"Gay," Bryson said. "Lesbo is lesbian, Ricki."

"What do you mean no one is gay? That's not true. Ellen is gay, and so is one of my friends. Well, not my friend, but her daddies. She has two dads."

"Who?"

"Maddie. That was one of her daddies in the store."

"Where?"

"On the other aisle," Rick said, flabbergasted, starting to walk away as if on a mission to find the gay daddy.

"Rick. Come back. Grandpa just texted. He'll be on his way soon."

In the checkout lane, Rick busied himself with lining up the groceries onto the conveyer belt. Everything had an order and place. Cheese and meat and milk. Frozen peas and french fries. Cardboard boxes and cans.

Audrey flicked hair from Bryson's eye.

"Stop, Mom."

"You know, Bryson, what we talked about earlier..."

"Mom," he said under his breath, looking around. "I'll talk about this stuff with Dad, okay. I'm sorry I asked."

"That's what I'm worried about," she whispered, barely moving her mouth.

Bryson's father would never get around to *the* conversation. Or conversations. Because Bryson knew about sex. *Penis meet Vagina.* But he didn't understand relationships. Dell might shove a porno mag or Cosmopolitan into her son's hands and consider the entire life talk over and done with. God, maybe she should send Bryson to a therapist.

"I just want you to know..." she began, ignoring the scowl on Bryson's face, "that what's important is how we treat each other. Okay? People have different ... well, they have various ways of experiencing..."

"Mom..."

"So long as people are safe and careful and practice with consenting adults, we don't pass judgment."

Audrey was beginning to sound like an Afterschool Special. At least she was having *the talk* or any talk ... or trying to open up some form of communication. Who knew what the boys he hung with at school discussed. She didn't want to remember her own prepubescent sexual initiation.

"Do boys ... well, your friends, how do they view girls or women?"

"I know how to respect a girl."

Sometimes, she forgot he was only twelve. Always talking like a little man.

"Respecting her means listening, too. Going outside your own comfort zone."

"Paper or plastic?" the clerk interrupted.

Bryson rolled his eyes and huffed out a dramatic, "Thank God."

Audrey playfully gave him a shove and told him to go after his brother. Rick had migrated toward the movie-dispensing machine and was tapping at the screen.

"How are you today, ma'am?"

Ma'am. When had that happened? Clerks used to card her for a bottle of wine, and now she was a ma'am.

Life was too short.

Today a ma'am. Other nights a vessel. Treated with consenting respect by a man some might say deserved no honor. These people at the supermarket — maybe even her own children once they grew older — might never understand. Even the gay Catholic daddy might not understand why she needed to be humiliated and bound, burned and used. Her ex-husband certainly didn't comprehend it. Still.

And did any of that matter? Did she need approval? Audrey didn't have to answer to any of them. Did God approve?

Could Audrey continue to straddle a line Gavin hadn't even defined? No contract. No collar. Few intimate conversations. No handholding.

"Ma'am?"

"Hmm?" She feigned a smile.

"Your total today is $112.34."

14

"Your lipstick is smeared," Kate said, placing her pinky on Audrey's mouth and fixing it. "There. All better." She held her gaze, and something in it lit Audrey from the inside.

"You know he'll make you take all this shit off," Kate said, referring to the paint, not the clothing. "Although ... that may go too."

"I don't care. Tonight ... I'm wearing it."

Kate raised both eyebrows. "Looking for a little extra incentive?"

"Maybe."

"Mom, I can't find my tablet," Bryson said as he banged on the locked door.

"Jesus, Bry, you scared the crap out of me." She eyed Kate and smiled. They both stifled a laugh. "Is Grandpa here yet?"

"No," he replied through the closed door. "You said we had to hurry home."

"He'll be here any second. Go look on the bookshelf for the contraption."

"Device, Mom. Jeez. I did."

"Honey, I'm getting ready."

"Well, Rick had it, and he won't tell me anything. I know he lost it. He always takes my things."

Without warning, Kate opened the door and stared down at the twelve-year-old young man, but she didn't have to look far. Kate was probably only about five-four, and Bryson was tall for his age. Brown hair and green eyes and the longest fucking eyelashes. He was a perfect mix of Audrey and Dell.

"We'll be out soon," Kate said, sporting a charming smile. "Shoo."

Bryson glanced at his mother, rolled his eyes, and then the doorbell rang.

"See who it is first," Audrey yelled after him.

"Mom ... jeez, you know it's Grandpa."

Kate shut the door, locked it, and started thumbing through dresses hanging in Audrey's closet.

"I'm wearing this," Audrey said, indicating the black skirt and top she already had on. "Don't even start with me."

"Are you wearing underwear?"

"Are you my Dom now?"

Kate sauntered toward Audrey, a smattering of giggles plastered across her face.

"Don't." Audrey pointed the mascara stick toward her friend, but Kate ignored the directive and inched up Audrey's skirt anyway. She whistled and smacked Audrey's bare ass ... probably for good measure.

"Feeling a little frisky tonight?"

"Always," Kate said and pressed her freshly painted lips together. "Hey, does your dad know where we go?"

"No, and don't you dare even hint at anything, especially in front of my—"

"Babies..."

"Stop it." Audrey's hand grazed the handle of the door.

"Wait."

"What?" She peered over her shoulder, unable to avoid the look in Kate's eyes as she stepped closer. Once they met face to face, Kate cupped Audrey's cheeks.

"Katy..."

"I don't want to mess up your face," she said and nuzzled her nose and then her cheeks. "You smell amazing."

Audrey exhaled and then met Kate's punch-drunk eyes.

"Please, soon. Tonight," Kate pleaded, the longing on the tip of her tongue. "This is the one thing he won't push you into. He won't spring it on you. He may never even ask."

"Ask me what?"

"He hasn't said anything?"

"In case you haven't noticed, Mr. Open Communication hasn't exactly been completely open."

"He will be. He must not think you're ready. He has his ways." Kate shrugged.

"Ready for what?"

"Forget it. Let's go."

"No. You implied something quite specific. You said the *one thing*. What's the thing, Kate?"

"I want you," Kate said, like a giant piece of bubble gum had just popped all over her face.

"That's not what you were going to say."

"Not verbatim." Kate flashed a wicked grin. "Look, Audrey, I love Peyton. And I love Gav like the bestest friend ever, and I love you too."

"You said you were pan, not total poly. You guys give me headaches."

Kate giggled. "I trust you, and I feel amazing when I'm around you. Don't you feel connected?"

"What if...?" Audrey shifted her eyes. "What if it ruins this? Our friendship? *This* is more important to me."

As Kate brushed her lips over Audrey's, giving her the

slightest peck, Audrey closed her eyes and exhaled, and then Kate stepped away.

"It won't. It will only get better. I promise you. It's a game, baby girl. We can all play together. I know we'll *play* very well together, and we all win. No one loses."

"Mom!" Rick yelled. "Bryson punched me in the arm!"

"Hold on."

"No, Mom," Rick said through the closed door. "Grandpa won't help me."

"All right. I'll be out in a minute."

"That's what you always say. Girls take freaking forever."

"Watch your mouth, Rick."

"You're going to steal his breath tonight," Kate interjected, and then Audrey opened the bathroom door. "He'll want to share you with everyone — or no one. Hard to tell with Gavin sometimes. He's a sadistic son of a bitch."

"Shhh," Audrey said, finger to her lips as she walked into the living room in her four-inch heels, a weekender over her shoulder.

"Dad, you have the numbers. Bry's inhaler—"

"Bean, I've been taking care of them since they were—"

"I know. I know. I can't help it."

"Must you girls always go to Tampa?"

"Tampa?" Rick piped up. "I wanna go to Tampa. Mom, the zoo is there, right? Take me with you."

"We're meeting friends tonight," Kate said with too much innuendo.

Dad only rolled his eyes. Maybe that was where Bryson picked it up — a habit she couldn't blame on Dell.

"No place for kids, Ricki," Audrey's father said with a ruffle of his grandson's hair.

Rick scoffed and squirmed and generally protested the way he did best. "Take me with you."

"Bryson, why are you looking at me like that?" Audrey had turned her attention to her older son.

Bryson screwed up his face, his expression saying *ewww*. "Why do you have on so much makeup?"

"Told ya," Kate chimed in.

"I'll be back Sunday night, Dad."

"Kate too?" Rick asked. "Will she stay the night? Please."

Lately, that had become a thing. Popcorn and a movie and Katy staying the night. Audrey couldn't keep sharing her bed with a woman who had just professed *I want you*. Could she? And what might her boys think? Bryson already knew Kate was bi. They wouldn't be able to wrap their heads around the labels poly or pan. Audrey was still trying to figure all of it out.

Audrey was still trying to figure out Audrey.

And what if Gavin pushed her into playing a scene with a woman? He hadn't yet, but that didn't mean he wouldn't. And even if he did, it didn't mean she was attracted to women, did it?

Gavin and Audrey still hadn't had a lengthy discussion of limits — the man really did break all his own rules. They didn't have what most people considered a traditional "relationship." They didn't take walks or hold hands.

Still, she trusted him. She felt connected to him.

Flowers and pillow talk and "normal" were the things she'd had for years. And right now, all she wanted was passion and risk and submission. She craved Gavin Sellers' dominance, his strong arms and soft lips, the way he pushed and pulled ... the irreplaceable cadence of his commands.

But was he grooming her for something bigger? The something — no, the *one thing* — Kate had referred to in the bathroom?

Fantasies came and went ... yet Kate remained.

Audrey *had* thought about Kate...

What her breasts would feel like in her hands. What her

nipples would taste like. How it would feel to slip her tongue inside her mouth. How Kate's head would look as Gavin forced it between Audrey's legs.

Fantasies weren't a snapshot of real life though.

Fantasies could be contained.

This was spilling over into the movie seats.

She needed the friendship.

Audrey couldn't blur any more lines.

Wishing for the moon, then being handed the universe came with risk. Supplication meant understanding what you sought, knowing you needed it and could handle it.

Fate didn't hold the cards — Audrey did.

An ace. A king. And a queen.

Kate had called it a game.

Audrey now called it reality.

And she didn't know how much longer she could straddle the fence between the two dimensions.

15

"I'm lost here," Audrey said inside the confines of one of the dungeon's six private rooms, one of the two without a viewing window.

Kate had insisted this was where Peyton wanted them to wait. And a good sub listened. Audrey had yet to see Gavin. They'd only just arrived. Audrey had drunk too much before the drive, and now she regretted it — regretted even coming, leaving the boys ... again.

"No, you're found." Kate stepped closer. "I found you." She sat next to Audrey at the end of the bed.

"I found you," Audrey replied, and they both got a little teary-eyed. "I'm not sure who he is or what he needs."

"What brought all this on?"

"The drive. The wine. I don't know... I'm used to navigating a second or third date. Nothing here follows a pattern, yet there are all sorts of rules."

She paused, considering whether or not she should say her next words. But fuck it, Kate was the kind of friend Audrey had never had and desperately needed.

"I know he keeps things from me."

"And you from him."

"But I told him about the kids." As if that was all there was to share. Audrey was more than a mother. More than an ex-wife.

"The babies."

"God, Katy, they're hardly babies." She tried to look away but couldn't. Kate hadn't stopped fiddling with Audrey's hair.

The two of them had barely moved — knees bent over the quilt, breathing becoming increasingly shallower, eyes communicating feelings Audrey couldn't speak — from the bed which was placed smack in the center of a different white room. One she hadn't visited before. There was a doctors' exam table to their left, a clean sheet of paper ready, stirrups in place. Tools hung on the wall, doctor's things and kinky things. And a small metal cabinet on wheels was next to it, probably full of vibrators and plugs and lube.

Kate's touch made Audrey uncomfortable and comforted. The whole room made her feel that way. A tunnel she either had to follow by instinct for relief and escape or be trapped in.

She tingled. Her mouth felt parched. Her pussy began to throb with a sharp, dull ache.

"I'm starting to feel like I'm out of my element here."

"You're starting to think too much. When we met, you said you wanted to have an adventure."

"But I don't know what I'm doing, mixing my regular life with this one. Up until now, I'd only really done—"

"Vanilla?"

"Yeah." Audrey smiled, and then Kate cupped her cheeks.

"We just talked about that. And ... not true. You're a kinky little bitch."

Audrey laughed, and Kate dropped her hands.

"You did some shit with your husband."

"That hardly counts."

"It does. You've known who you are for a while, babe. But it's always scary when it's time to come out."

Audrey stared at Kate, her mouth still dry, her mind racing with thoughts. She'd known she was different for years. She knew exactly what she craved from a partner, but she'd tried over and over to deny it. It wasn't just sexual.

"And now you're a pro. You've watched me. You've been doing scenes with Gavin. He's had you in a couple of these rooms and on the cross. He took your ass in the first main chamber in front of everyone."

"You were there?"

"Of course." Kate leaned closer until their noses practically touched. Audrey could smell her cinnamon mints and shampoo. "Kiss Kitten Katy. I wanted you earlier ... so much ... in your fucking bathroom."

Gavin's expectations pulsed through Audrey's veins along with ... the "one thing" Kate had mentioned and the need to define these "relationships" or set boundaries. Society's thumb was strangling her ... but still ... she wanted to know what Kate tasted like, wanted to know how she would kiss. Soft or hard? Bruising? Needy? She imagined the feel of her tongue.

"This isn't cheating, Audrey. Only sharing, love, connection."

"I still need to ask his permission first."

The desire to do so was pure instinct. She craved a Master/Dominant/partner who *wanted* to be asked and then who would subsequently relish granting her wishes — giving her, sharing her, owning her. But ... Audrey still wasn't certain she was ready for sex with a woman — with her friend.

Fuck ... everything was still muddled, warring with common sense.

"Does *he*?"

"What do you mean?"

Kate sighed her dramatic sigh and pulled at the ends of Audrey's dirty-blonde hair, twisting the curls around her fingers.

"Have you thought about touching a woman, Audrey? Have you thought about—?"

"I need to ask—"

"I know, but they'll want to scene, babe. I want you to myself."

"*They*?"

Kate didn't reply, but Audrey knew she referred to Gavin *and* Peyton. Audrey's head spun.

"Why now?" Audrey was never more aware of the rise and fall of their chests. "I need—"

"Please..."

Kate's fingers threaded through Audrey's hair. And as their breasts pressed closer together — Audrey's tiny ones and Kate's extremely large ones — Audrey could feel the heave, feel the hardening of Kate's nipples through her shirt, and she wanted to see them for herself, not in a room full of other gawkers. Not in her kitchen. She wanted those large, fantastic breasts all to herself.

She had thought of women.

The door opened. Both of them instinctively parted. Audrey went to the nearest wall and leaned against it for support while Peyton took stock of the entire situation, seeming not to miss a beat, his eyebrows raised.

"Kitty Kate, I asked you to wait. You'll rush this and ruin it for everyone."

Audrey's heart pumped into overdrive. *One thing ... to wait ... ruin this.* Maybe she was having a heart attack or an anxiety attack. Each breath felt like she'd just resurfaced from a deep dive without oxygen.

"I'm patient, sir. She's not afraid."

Peyton glanced over at what had to be only a semblance of a woman — Audrey — who'd begun to slide down the wall. He caught her before she hit the floor or passed out, lifted her over his shoulder, and brought her to the bed.

"No!" Audrey yelled. She fought, struggled, beat her fists into his shoulder blades. "No!"

"I'm not going to touch you." He laid her on the quilt. "Shhh. Stop being a brat."

He grabbed her wrists — apparently full of shit about not touching her — and held them above her head, pinning them to the mattress.

Her eyes must've gone black, and the fucking ache — the tingly sensations and loss of her moral compass — returned. She looked at Kate, then at Peyton. Kate to Peyton.

And then Peyton kissed her...

"Fuck, Peyt," Kate said in an achy clip, joining him at the end of the bed — Kate still standing, Peyton on his knees straddling Audrey, both watching her, perhaps waiting for her to kick or scream or cry.

"Where is he?" Audrey asked, drugged on the anticipation of being at the mercy of the two, being pushed and used.

Peyton and Kate shared a meaningful look.

"Enough with the secrets. *Where is he*?"

"Aftercare, Audrey," Peyton answered.

"What?" she asked, and Peyton released her wrists, stood, and fingered his messy, sunset-streaked locks. "Alone?"

"I was with him. I cared for him. He's sleeping."

Have you been hurt with a cane?

Yes.

You've submitted? Who?

Her fingers caressed her lips, and her eyes glossed over as she stared at the ceiling, considering a memory, Gavin's words, trying to put pieces together, but nothing fit ... yet.

"I want to see him."

"He may not want to see you. You were supposed to come tomorrow."

"Kate texted you."

"I didn't tell him."

"Why?"

"Maybe it's time to put an end to secrets." Peyton moved to the couch, and Kate wasted no time kneeling at his feet. "Sometimes Gavin needs pushing too."

He already had Kate's top off and bra up. Some of his fingers tweaked a nipple while others threaded through the strands of her coal-black hair. Kate looked beyond tranquil — a picture waiting to be painted or captured. Audrey knew what Kate felt between her thighs, knew what went through her mind — nothing. And nothing was a powerful and dangerous drug. They didn't need anything synthetic. They had *this*.

Peyton tapped the seat beside him while glaring at Audrey.

Audrey glanced at her friend's tits. "I want to see him."

Peyton tapped the seat again.

Audrey imagined every scenario she possibly could. The repercussions of following Peyton's command. The repercussions of disobeying. The fallout from either situation. Or she could just go home.

She hated to admit this ... but home had lost its original meaning. The thing you feel when you have dinner together with family at the designated table. The place you come to after giving birth at the hospital.

Her "home" had been broken by divorce.

Maybe she wasn't cut out for either life. Kinky or straight. She couldn't have sex and submit without feeling a million little feelings, without asking big philosophical questions, and she couldn't lie under a husband and dream about being used and bound and collared, sometimes faking an orgasm, then roll over and go to sleep feeling empty and lonely.

Where was the middle?

Where was the light?

And what path was she supposed to take?

16

Audrey left the pheromone-filled room, walked the halls, and went up to the other five remaining doors. *Gavin must be in his room* she thought ... although he'd never admitted to living there. And she'd only been there once.

Had she ever seen Gavin's naked backside, the rear of his thighs? Did he have scars? Was he a switch? Who was he?

Sounds came from room number one. Peyton and Kate were in six. And the remaining four had windows.

Turning on her heels, she decided to head to the bar. She took a seat, tapped her nails across the granite, and waited. Breathed. Tried to stop imagining his pain. His needs. Empathy had always been her biggest fault.

"Do you want a drink, kid?" Darcy asked, and Audrey jumped. "Fuck. I didn't mean to scare you." She laughed.

Audrey watched Darcy twist her hair into a high ponytail — this week it was blonde with purple streaks — and as she lifted her hair, the tats on her neck became visible. Nipple rings poked through the material of her shirt. And the frames of her glasses matched her highlights.

"Peyton said ... he's in ... Gavin is..."

"Ahhh..." Darcy sighed, tossing a rag over her shoulder while reading the palm of Audrey's eyes. "When did you fall for him?" Darcy tapped the tip of Audrey's nose with an acrylic fingernail.

Sucking her lower lip into her mouth, Audrey folded her arms across her chest and glanced away.

"Advice, kid?"

"You mean besides the standard — don't ask Gavin questions..."

"Yeah, yeah, yeah..." Darcy teased, then became serious. "Don't ever fall in love with a switch."

Bodhi was *not* the place Audrey had expected to frequent, then fall in love. But misconceptions were abundant, and she found she was often wrong when it came to her perceptions of what occurred inside these decadent walls.

Darcy exhaled and put a full glass of wine on the bar. "You like red, yeah?" She pushed it closer.

Audrey slid it back. "I need to see him."

Darcy focused on something over Audrey's shoulder. And Audrey could see his reflection in the mirror. Behind her stood a man. A tired and worn man. Or was he always tired? Always worn? Had she only seen what she'd wanted to? Taken only what she needed?

As much as Audrey had thought she was ready to talk to Gavin — *communicate* — she'd had a change of heart.

Standing with haste, she attempted to turn from his polarizing Copenhagen gaze. But he caught her elbow, gripping it as though he were keeping her from slipping over the edge of a tall mountain.

"Let me go," she whispered.

"You don't want that." Where her voice had been harsh, his was kind. Too kind. Filled with care and heart and pain.

"You want to know everything ... I want to know everything," she snarled, "but all we seem to do is hurt and fuck."

"Not here." He glanced around the nearly empty room. Darcy had made herself scarce.

"Where then? *Aftercare*?" So much for the full tour, full disclosure, and open communication.

Breaking free from his grasp, she began to head for the exit. But he caught her again, and this time, he utilized his infamous chokehold to restrict her movement.

Pressing his broad chest against her backside, he placed his mouth at her ear and whispered, "Stay. There's a reason for all this."

Wasn't that what she always told her boys? Except it was a lie. There was no reason for any of it. Feelings were lies.

"You've been grooming me. Using me. You want all of us to fuck. Kate told me. Then Peyton scolded her for *rushing* it. Am I a plan, Gavin? *What are you all to each other*? Where do I fit? I can't do this. I thought I could. I know you want to share me with others, but this ... Kate is my friend—"

"Kate's your friend who you want to fuck."

"Fuck you."

"You've watched her submit, and I've watched you."

"It's fantasy, Gavin. Don't you know the difference? What people daydream about isn't always what they want. Put any sane person—"

"Careful, Audrey."

"That's not what I mean. Put someone ... a vanilla person ... in a room to watch people fuck, and chances are they're going to get hard and wet. They might want to participate. But take those same people out of the room, and some won't be able to live with themselves afterward. They don't know what to do with that. *With this world*. I'm in between." Her lungs rattled from speaking so frantically, so fast, causing her words to sound jarred. "Don't you see?" She inhaled, willing herself to calm. "I'm the piece that doesn't belong."

He turned her around before she finished speaking the last word. Taking her in his arms, he held her, wrapped those fucking fantastic biceps around her, secured her, and whispered in her ear.

"You're the piece. The centerpiece. The sacrifice. The reason."

She cried into his chest, released a thousand tears no one else in her life had time for.

"Before you came here, I..." he began, and she stopped crying, kept her ear against his T-shirt, and listened to his heartbeat. "I stopped taking this seriously. I often refused to top. And long before that"—Gavin looked around, probably to ensure they were still alone—"there was a girl ... Harper..."

Audrey remained captive in his arms and with his story as she pulled her head back to gaze directly upon him.

"Did you love her?"

"Yes, Audrey. I beat her, humiliated her, loved her, collared her, and she..." He looked away. His starry-night eyes were glistening. "One day ... Darcy found her. She'd hung herself." Gavin's throat bobbed as he met Audrey's gaze. "Members wanted to believe she'd asphyxiated. That it was some kind of kinky sex game. We experimented with breath play, but I was certain she wouldn't do it alone. I did some digging, found out she'd been on pills. The list of side effects was as long as my arm."

"It wasn't your fault."

"It didn't matter, baby girl. This is my place. My rules. My responsibility. Then I met Peyton..."

"Show me," she whispered, staring into his eyes with a sincerity she hoped he couldn't deny.

Feigning a smile, he tugged on her hair and then on her arm. She followed him to a room, down a long hallway, beyond the bar.

He flicked on a light and said, "You've been through here before."

It was a gym. Apparently, where the man honed those fucking godly arms.

"I don't remember."

"Because you were flying."

He led her through another door and into a tiny room — the only one in the club with ambience, character, and multiple colors. She'd been here the night he'd given her a bath. The night he'd claimed her ass. The night he'd told her about Hannah. Flying on the way into his hideaway and head bowed on the way out.

In addition to the pictures and books she'd noticed the first time, there were also implements of pleasure (or pain) lining one wall — some tools she'd never seen before — placed next to Jesus on the crucifix. The smell of candles, wax, and smoke lingered in the air. The bed was made but looked rumpled. She recalled there being no windows but had failed to notice the floor. It was concrete, painted with many beautiful colors, all in swirl patterns.

He knelt on a small rug, took off his shirt, and bowed his head.

"Gavin..."

"Touch me," he whispered.

At first, standing behind him and over him, she only looked at the sores, the scars, the map of his body she longed to discover. She studied his topography for an eternity.

Then ... she touched him.

Her fingers instinctively stopped on the tattoo in the middle of his shoulder blades. She traced the dark ink, beginning with what looked like a letter G followed by three V symbols — only the first was sideways, its point facing right. The second one was upside down and the third was normal. In between each letter or symbol was imagery, drawings. The G held water, the first V, the sun. The second V held water and the third a tall mountain.

"It means 'God is greater than our highs and lows.'" His voice and breath shook. "I had it done after Harper died and when Michael no longer wanted anything to do with me."

Audrey's fingers stopped for a moment over the intricate pattern on his skin. *His son no longer wanted anything to do with him?* His body looked so certain, so squared, so full of confidence, but inside she knew there were trails, miles of heartbreak.

Next, she traced the edges of the welts and bruises while he held stock still, only his muscles flexing from the act of breathing. His beautiful soul tickled her fingertips, his honesty something she could capture and keep forever like a cherished photograph.

Why did she want this type of damage? Need it? And on him, it stood for something else. On him, these scars and welts and bruises couldn't be the same innate need — this couldn't be *her* need. And the man who fulfilled her desires so perfectly couldn't be on the receiving end of this same kind of pain.

Could he?

She wanted to protect him from pain the way he protected her by inflicting it. But maybe that was why he needed it too.

Dropping her hands to her sides, she inhaled, then watched as he pulled on his shirt and stood.

"You're a switch?"

"I'm not defined," he said as he ran a knuckle across her cheek.

"But you need this?"

"Sometimes."

"Why?" she asked even though she knew the answer. Submission and pain meant she was safe in the care of her partner.

"Why do you need it, Audrey? Why did you leave your mundane life?"

"I didn't leave it. My kids aren't mundane."

"That's not what I meant. You have a foot in both worlds. One here..." He paused and stared at the door. "And one out there with the others."

"Gavin, my kids require it."

"I have something for you. I wasn't sure you were ready, but, like most things between us, I've decided it's no longer my decision."

He opened the single drawer in the small table next to the bed. A square black box, rather large and flat, was in his hands. Audrey's fingers instinctively went to her neck, but her thoughts went to her sons.

Motherhood had drawn her closer to her children but farther from herself. And Gavin, he slept here ... in this room. He lived here. His entire life revolved around kink, and Audrey ... she still didn't know her own place.

After opening the box, Gavin placed the jewelry around Audrey's neck, then guided her to the mirror across from the bed and over the dresser. She *had* imagined this moment many times, the way another girl might've imagined her wedding.

Palm flat against the front of the collar, she gazed at herself in the mirror. It was silver and looked more like a necklace. Fringe hung from the chain, but there was a loop and a lock in the rear, under her hair, and he had just clicked it into place.

His Copenhagen eyes turned gray, dark. The feelings they couldn't always explain or justify filled the room, sucking out all the oxygen.

It was only him.

Only her.

And this collar.

This symbol of archaic belonging.

Swallowing, she met his eyes in the antique oval mirror and invited him into her kingdom of not having a place or every piece to the puzzle. She said *yes* with her eyes and breath. And he heard every word she silently uttered.

"Sometimes there's a public ceremony when a Master collars his slave, but I wanted this to be between only us tonight."

And she agreed.

She might've once wished for some sort of formality, something akin to what Kate had described between her and Peyton, but this moment surpassed her imagination because what she felt for Gavin was more important than having witnesses or wearing pretty things. These words between them now would be their vows, their commitment.

"We'll inform others later." He glanced at her neck. "This means I own you. We make our own rules. But *you are my submissive.*"

Gavin had said he'd collared the girl who'd taken her own life. She knew he didn't take this step lightly. And neither did she. She pushed away the nagging voice reminding her they hardly knew each other and focused again on the feelings. The love Darcy had intuited. And she shoved aside all thoughts of Gavin and Peyton, his revelation ... what it all meant. Did the men fuck each other too?

"You already own me," she said as he trailed a finger from her tailbone to her nape and tugged on the loop.

"Yes," he said above a whisper, his voice cracking.

"What if I want more?" Tears laced her tone. "What if I want to be with regular people?"

"Regular people," he said on a tight laugh. "You're free to see others. Open communication first. Honesty. I would never keep you from others. But *regular* people won't share *you with me.* And I will always have you. One foot here..."

Sighing, she dropped her chin toward the floor. "You will

never be in my other life?" She hadn't meant to say those words in the form of a question — or out loud.

"You mean, will I meet your children, have romantic dinners with you? No, Audrey. You're my property. I will protect you, see to your every need, assign you tasks, but I won't insert myself somewhere I'm *not* needed."

"But..."

"I won't be part of society as you are. I married at eighteen, divorced at twenty-one. Michael rarely speaks to me anymore. He's a Christian who takes every word of scripture quite literally. According to him, I'm an apostate. And that's his label because *here* in *this world*, the world where you dip your toes and only get one foot wet — this is where *I am me*."

He tugged on her hair in succession — one, two, three.

"You wish for me to only wear this here?" She grazed her fingers along the edges.

"Yes. But I don't *wish*. If you accept it, then you'll be *expected* to wear it. There will be consequences if you don't. You may keep it on your person. We'll both have a key. But the moment you enter my building, you will have it on, and you won't take it off again until you leave."

"Please, sir." A carnal begging flooded her tone.

"Please, what, baby girl?"

"Own me. Please. Use me for your pleasure and make me your property."

Placing his index finger inside the circle on the collar, he dragged her by her neck to the floor, opened his pants, and shoved his cock into her mouth. She choked and sputtered. He yanked harder on the collar and thrust forward.

"Suck," he moaned. "Take it."

Pulling her head off him for only a second to demand she breathe, he then shoved his full length into her mouth again and groaned louder than she'd ever heard him groan before.

Spit spilled from the sides of her mouth as he used her hole for his own pleasure, causing her lips to swell, her jaw to ache. Every few seconds, he allowed her to breathe, but each time he reentered her mouth, it was with more violence. She felt like she was in a military line, obeying strict orders, constricted but freed in his clutches, filled with his cock and safe with his collar pinching her neck.

Closing her eyes, the eager sounds of her feasting increased as he pumped her face, balls slapping her chin. And she wanted all of him, more of him, wanted his balls in her mouth along with his cock, wanted to suck him off until it made her faint or gag or vomit.

She would die for him.

Maybe the other girl, the one he loved, had hung herself *for him*.

Sacrificed her life for him.

Audrey's death would be the ultimate freedom.

And then Gavin pulled out, and she regained her senses, her logic, her maternal instincts. She wanted to live, wanted to soak in his cum ... and she did.

He released over her lips and her cheeks and her chin, and then he smeared it all over her face, rubbed his semen into the collar and underneath it. Finally, after pulling her to her feet, he stroked his cum-covered thumb across her bottom lip, dipping it into her mouth as she sucked the taste from him.

"I love you, Audrey," he said, his eyes transfixed, otherworldly, possessed. "But don't confuse my love for store-bought romance. I'm not your husband. Not even your lover. I'm your owner. *You will obey my every fucking command*," he hissed.

And then, after wiping her face with his shirt, he kissed her, cupped her cheeks, bit her bottom lip until it bled ... until she sobbed against his mouth and sagged against his chest.

A few minutes later, he laid her on the bed. *His bed*. He told her she would need her strength because soon she would make her debut as his pet, his submissive, his property.

She would not refuse him.

King would never fall from her lips.

Even if it meant Kate and Peyton and Gavin would all have their way, each of them filling a hole, all but the one in her chest, she'd learn to live with it — the other side of denial.

Lust would be her penchant.

17

The merits of having a man around:

He could go on the roof and clean and unclog the lint trap.

He could load the dishwasher the wrong way.

Kill spiders in the bathtub.

Assemble furniture.

Board windows for an approaching storm.

He could lie in bed and welcome a woman's center over his groin, straddling him, taking him inside her.

Except ... he wasn't exceptional at any of those things. She did the cleaning, the washing. She usually instigated the fucking. And he didn't like to call it *that* feral word.

Dell didn't like any of the really good words. *Cunt, fuck, bitch.*

This was marriage.

Or it used to be.

Had been.

Has been.

Over.

She wiped the back of her hand across her forehead, her fingers sudsy and sticky from the gunk on the plates and cups. The kids were in bed. Maybe they were even sleeping. And if she were lucky, she would get a few minutes alone without the possibility of a disturbance before she slipped into her own bed.

She wore the collar at night as she slept and thought of him — the man who had no interest in being a husband, only an owner.

The silence had never felt so good.

18

Protocol for their relationship had to be discussed. Their *relationship* had to be discussed ... period. How had they come this far and not laid out their expectations? Gavin's came in the form of whispers and bondage and now ... the collar.

He finally explained, during the next weekend she came to him, what he normally expected of his submissive: 24/7 control in most aspects of his slave's life. But he told her that due to their unique circumstances, adjustments would have to be made.

"Everything about this is new to me," he said from the confines of his private room. He sat in a chair near the couch and bookshelf. Audrey stood near the door. Darcy had just deposited her there. "You're on the outside. You have limitations."

It didn't matter how many times she'd already insisted otherwise, he didn't accept her weekend-only visits as promise of servitude.

Yet, he'd collared Audrey.

He owned Audrey.

The lock across her heart proved it.

Did he feel it whenever they were apart?

"Darcy once told me you break all your own rules."

"With you, I find myself writing all new ones. Come." He nodded at the swirls of paint on the concrete floor.

She kneeled, relaxing into the posture they both needed, and rested her head on his thigh.

"I love you, Audrey."

In the pause between that declaration and the next, Audrey had become nimble, pliable, her breathing like one of a small child taking comfort in the arms of a trusted parent.

"What won't you do for me?" he said while stroking her hair. She imagined the look on his face: utter power mixed with a strained vulnerability. She released more air from her lungs.

"Don't ever tickle my feet, sir." Her lips curved against his thigh, and she sensed his own smile filling the room. She didn't need to look up at him or move to be sure of its presence.

"Should we make a list?"

She shook her head, pressing her cheeks and lips against his jeans.

"Audrey..." His voice sounded pained with lust and love as he gripped strands of sandy hair from under her neck.

"There's nothing I won't do, Master."

"That's not true."

"Don't ask me to choose."

In a split second, he jerked her chin upward, forcing her to lock onto his stark gaze. "I don't feel the need to continually remind you that I would never ask you to choose. You should feel that when I restrain you. When I hurt you. Everything's a lesson. What I expect of you will be things you can always fulfill."

Tears filled her eyes. She inclined her head against the comfort of his body again.

"I will assign you tasks outside these walls, and you must follow them to the letter."

Audrey gathered up what little give she could find in his jeans and bunched the material in her fists. "Yes, sir."

"None of what I ask or expect should burden you. And I trust you'll inform me of such feelings if they occur."

The physical and spiritual response Audrey had to his words was strange ... or maybe it was normal. It was erotic without any need for nudity. The nakedness was in their hearts. The words he spoke and the prospect she could please him even when they would be apart filled her with an indescribable hope.

"Tell me about your routines."

Content to lie at his feet all afternoon, Audrey regaled him with details. Work schedule. School schedules. Extracurricular schedules. Errands.

"Do you have time for yourself?" he asked when she'd finished.

"This is time for me. Here."

"Your first task will be to meditate."

Her face must've been a sight because Gavin laughed. Audrey blushed.

"Already balking. Would you like me to paddle you?"

She stifled a groan but couldn't stop the sharp sensation traveling through her groin. She'd never before felt she could orgasm from such subtle instigations. This was the true beginning of her dream. The sex and bondage and pain had only been a prelude. This was what she wanted, needed, craved. Gavin had been right to make her wait. The months of coming here had prepared her for this new level of service.

"Go to the shelf. Bring me the Bible."

It wasn't just *the* Bible; it was his. *Gavin Sellers* was engraved in gold lettering on the front. The traditional black cover felt like soft-bound leather. It smelled like him. And its size was what Audrey would've described as medium. It had both heft and weightlessness.

"Undress," he said, taking the book from her hands. He waited for her to slip off her jeans and shirt and shoes. "When I call you into my private room or ask you to wait for me in here, you are to present yourself to me, nude and positioned this way." He guided her to her knees and proceeded to adjust her as though she were a wooden doll with joints he could bend and twist.

Knees spread shoulder-width apart.

Eyes trained on the floor.

Breasts out.

Arms to her sides, wrists forward, palms open.

"Never wear jeans in my presence. Only skirts or dresses. And as you ready yourself to leave to come to me on the weekend, you're to send me a text message first and await instructions. I'll have a few other things to share with you later as well." A pause followed, and then he lifted her chin, met her eyes, and said, "Answer me, Audrey."

"Yes, sir." Joy spread through her poised body. She had to bite back a smile.

"If it pleases me." The same held-back smile lit Gavin's eyes too.

"Yes, sir. If it pleases you."

Reaching a hand between her legs, he slid two fingers down her seam, causing her eyelids to flutter and her mouth to part. She wasn't sure just how wet she'd become during their conversation until he lifted his fingers and showed her the effect he'd had on her. He painted her lips with her juices, and then he wiped the remainder on his jeans.

"You please me, baby girl. Always. Stay in ready position while I read ... and think about why I chose this passage."

After opening the Bible to a page appearing to belong in Revelation, he began to read without paying her any mind. Except, even in his seeming disregard, she was under his thumb.

Nothing escaped his eye. Audrey was a squirming, wanton ball of need.

"'Then I heard another voice from heaven say: 'Come out of her, my people,' so that you will not share in her sins, so that you will not receive any of her plagues; for her sins are piled up to heaven, and God has remembered her crimes. Give back to her as she has given; pay her back double for what she has done. Pour her a double portion from her own cup. Give her as much torment and grief as the glory and luxury she gave herself. In her heart she boasts, 'I sit enthroned as queen. I am not a widow; I will never mourn.' Therefore in one day her plagues will overtake her: death, mourning and famine. She will be consumed by fire, for mighty is the Lord God who judges her.'"

Gavin read the verses the way he did most things: controlled, precise, no fuss. He asked her not to speak as he returned the Bible to its place on the shelf with the other books. Books on the art of Kinbaku. Books about infidelity and monogamy. Religious and spiritual titles. She hadn't had time to observe all of the them.

Audrey hadn't moved from her ready position. Her limbs ached. Her thighs felt sticky. Still, he made her wait while he did other tasks. When he finally came back to her side, he had lube in one hand and her panties in the other.

After preparing her body for his assault and stuffing the lace into her mouth, he positioned her on all fours, grabbed her hips, and shoved his dick into her ass, taking her roughly over the hard and unforgiving floor.

She imagined what they looked like. Beasts meeting in a field. Animals fucking with the basest of instincts. Savages.

Drool pooled down her chin, grunts came from her throat, and tears welled and poured from the brown of her eyes — muddy puddles of awareness — as peace settled over her consciousness ... a peace she could never, ever describe.

The closest thing to earthly Nirvana.

Flying through an open field of pain and pleasure and ownership.

"What does the scripture mean?" he snarled in her ear, his chest against her back, her small breasts scraping the floor. His dick had just finished pulsing its seed inside the tight hole meant only for him.

I'm the only one who will fill this hole. Do you understand? I will share you on my terms. I'll give you plenty of cock to suck, but no one — no one — will fuck this place. Ever. Mine... Mine... Mine...

Sucking back a sob, her heart on the surface of her skin, Gavin removed the panties from her mouth, and before she could even catch her breath, she said, "It means God is the judge." The cry she had held back released from her lungs. "This isn't a sin. I've left Babylon and found something religion denies."

19

Saturday night, he led her to a room. A private one. The one he'd first locked her inside of. She wore his collar. He didn't or wouldn't hold her hand as they made their way through the crowds. She'd expected that but not what was on the other side of the door.

Three men sat on the bed, blindfolded. Hands behind their backs. Naked. She couldn't tell if their wrists were bound or they were simply compliant. She wondered how long they'd been sitting there. She wondered how they were already hard.

Swallowing the largest lump of anticipatory fear and adrenaline, she gazed at Gavin, swallowed again, blinked, maybe breathed.

"Put on the items I set out in the bathroom, then return to me. Here." He nodded toward the foot of the bed where the three nude men sat. Each man shared similar features: dark hair shaved close to the scalp, abs taut and lean, tattoos ... and dicks standing at attention, waiting for release.

They were in the calm before the storm. Any one of them could've heard a pin drop. Each person waited for Gavin to make demands.

"Go," he said, eyeing her shaking hands. Gavin didn't flinch. His confidence forced her to place one foot in front of the other and move.

The bathroom contained three items:

One white tank top, a few sizes too small.

A white, lacy thong.

A pair of athletic knee-high socks.

Her hard nipples showed through the ribbed tank top. The formations (not cleavage) of her small breasts popped from the scoop, and the hem of the shirt inched way above her belly button. It had no stretch. Only give. The socks made her feel safe. The tightness. The length. The underwear bothered her. At thirty-five, she was beyond thongs. Never wore them. The string inside her crack aroused and irritated her — a double-edged sword.

Even though there were four of them out there, she only saw one man as she came back into the black-and-white room — Gavin. His eyes dark, his breath strong. The other men, the beautiful creatures whose eyes were hidden behind the blindfolds, whose hands were not in fact bound, took shallow breaths. No doubt Gavin had been the one keeping them hard, talking to them, commanding them, keeping them on that delicious edge he owned.

With a yank of Audrey's hair, he pulled her closer, then he gathered up her dirty-blonde locks, tying them high on her head in a ponytail.

"Face me," he growled low in her ear.

He tweaked her nipples repeatedly, and when she made the mistake of shifting her head to the right toward the men, he slapped her cheek. She groaned. He cupped her pussy.

"Mine," he hissed.

"Yes, sir."

He slapped her face again and commanded, "Don't speak."

Her breathing matched that of the creatures he wouldn't allow her to look upon. The shaking hadn't subsided, but the slaps reminded her she didn't need to be afraid. Gavin was in charge. She only had to obey.

He painted her lips red with a tube he pulled from his pocket. He went outside the lines, coloring around her mouth, pressing the lipstick to her skin until the slanted edge of it became blunt, then he grabbed the hair dangling from the pony holder and forced her to her knees on the floor.

"They're for you," he whispered, voice brimming with intention and power and heat. "I want to watch you. They won't come until I say. And neither will you. They can't touch you. They can't kiss you. You will suck them, and I will beat you, and then we will *all* come ... if you please me, baby girl." He pulled on her hair until her eyes blurred. "You will please me, won't you? Or do you want to use your *word*? Make it all go away?"

Gavin's pants strained. She could smell the arousal of both him and the other men she kneeled before. Sagging a little in his hold, she moaned and shook her head.

"You know that's not enough." He flicked his eyes to the bed. "Speak now. Tell them."

"I will please my Master. I will suck you ... all of you. I'll do whatever Master tells me to do."

The creatures' breathing patterns changed. They must've also been instructed not to speak. Their dicks looked painfully hard. Their faces looked equally wrinkled with aching expectation. She didn't want to know how long he'd kept them on the edge or why they obeyed. If she knew, she'd have to think and be logical, and she came here, she submitted to Gavin, so she wouldn't have to do any of that.

All she had to do was obey.

Gavin never released his hold. With her hair tight in his fist, he positioned her over each man in turn, forcing the rhythm, while he struck her with a wooden paddle. Paddles were his favorite tool. She wasn't allowed to bite down in the slightest on their cocks to transfer the pain. He disavowed the use of her hands. Sometimes, he also held their dicks, pumped them into her mouth, thrusting them so far into her throat she made gagging sounds. And he beat her, called her names, told her how beautiful she looked, how much she pleased him. Then after she'd sucked the three creatures for what felt like forever — because her jaw ached but she still wanted more, more, more — he ordered her to the floor, flat on her back, and told her to remove her tank top.

She didn't think she'd ever seen his eyes so wide, his pupils so dark, his chest heave so deeply. He looked like he would explode with lust. Kneeling with a knee on each side of her, his jeans pulled down so that his own cock sprung free, he wrote on her chest with the lipstick. She didn't need a mirror to know what he drew. She could feel each letter take shape. They were large, unmistakable. He started with an S just above her breasts and below her chin, followed by an L directly beneath it, then a U, and finally a T.

"Open," he said, slapping her mouth with his cock. He hit her cheeks with it first, then told her to lick and suck only the tip.

"You own this word." Slapping her face again with his dick, his eyes boring into hers, he then made her lick and suck. "You own their pleasure, and I own you. Do you want to come?"

She imagined this was what it was to be in a coma. She could only moan. She could hear and breathe, but she could only moan. It was like a dream. And it was ... a dream come true.

Standing with his cock in his hand, he pumped himself as he removed the blindfolds from the creatures and nodded in Audrey's direction, indicating they imitate him.

All four men stood above her, looking down while jerking

their lipstick-stained cocks toward her coma-induced body. She wanted the floor to swallow her up … or she wanted to drown in her lust, her need for this — the addiction her owner had created or awoken. Heat had pooled so deep inside her belly, her thighs and lower back, it cut through her skin and organs like the tip of a sharp blade.

Imagining the taste of the cum of the four men mixing on her tongue, the smell of them, she ached violently as she gazed up at them through hooded eyes, through a tunnel — she seemed to be on the other side of it. Audrey at one end, the four hard men at the other.

She was a slut.

Fuck, it was the only label she wanted, needed, and owned.

"So pretty," Gavin murmured.

He stood directly over her, a foot on each side of her waist. The other men stood at her sides. She made eye contact only with him. He watched her lids flutter, her breasts heave, and the bright red vertical letters all with what she felt was aroused adoration.

She *had* pleased him.

"So, so pretty," he whispered. He looked like he might cry — a tower of strength mixed with a vulnerability he couldn't contain.

And again, it was only the two of them, Audrey and Gavin, surrounded by lust and fascination, cravings most people would never understand.

"Come for me. Open your mouth. Stick out your tongue. Put your hand inside your panties." He paused, watching her palm slip past the letters and her fingers disappear.

"Together," he groaned. "Everyone." He glanced at the mystical, ethereal creatures. "We'll come together." He looked again at her, his voice aching with concern and determination. "It will rain on you."

The noises she made increased. The stroking she gave her clit and pussy lips intensified.

"No, no, no. Eyes open," he said, ripping her from deep space, from the carnal coma while pumping himself, fucking his fist. "Eyes on me. Good girl."

The three creatures released first, then he dropped to his knees, rubbed the tip of himself over the remaining red of her lips, and spilled over what they'd done. He smeared all the semen together over the whole of her chest, into the red letters, her breasts, under her chin and collar, and over her swollen lips.

Gavin and Audrey's gazes remained steadfast and locked onto each other as she began to convulse with her own monumental release. Squeezing her thighs together, she sobbed openly, unable to contain the shaking or emotions.

It was an adrenaline crash of epic proportions.

"Good girl," he whispered, wiping the sweat from her forehead. He continued to praise her over and over, quietly, his heart sounding as if it resided in his voice box. "Stay here, baby girl."

The moment he stood, her eyes closed from sheer exhaustion, yet her pussy still throbbed with its own heartbeat. Her head lolled to the side as she ascertained sounds: her Master's commands, jeans zipping, shirts being buttoned. Her senses seemed heightened. And then a door opened and closed, indicating three satisfied men had left the room.

Gavin returned with a basin of warm water and a washcloth, cleaned her off, massaged and oiled her butt cheeks, but said nothing. And she only lay there, eyes closed, thoughts far gone from anything resembling what she knew of this universe.

He brought her bottled water. Made her drink. Then he carried her to his private room where he took hold of her wrists, handcuffed them in front of her waist, clasped a chain to them, and led her to his bed.

"You have free rein of the studio. I'll feed you. Are you hungry?"

She shook her head.

"Audrey..." He tapped her cheek. "Why aren't you speaking now?"

Because she would cry again. Sob like a little girl. She shrugged, feeling her damn eyes water despite her efforts.

"What you just did, what we did — was beautiful." He slid his knuckle across her cheek. "Consensual."

"I know," she whispered, dropping her chin, biting her lip, squelching the tears.

"This is play, baby girl. A way to satisfy our needs. Do you trust me?"

She met his eyes with an awareness that seemed to make him take an internal step backward.

"Yes," she answered without any room for doubt or complacency. "I liked it," she continued, eyes still focused on his, searching deep into them and floating away in the pools of his blues as she suddenly remembered a lesson. A recent one. A single word he'd taught her that would forever change the directory of the way she navigated relationships.

"Compersion. Do you know what it means, Audrey?" he'd asked one night as they lay in his bed together.

"I've never heard it."

"Have you ever felt jealousy while watching me interact with people here?"

"No." She blushed. "But I haven't watched you ... be intimate with anyone."

"You've watched me teach, seen me paddle and flog and cane others. That's still a form of intimacy."

"I didn't feel jealous. What does it mean? The word."

"Did your husband exhibit jealousy?"

"Gavin..."

He ran his finger under her collar as she leaned into his touch.

"Ex," she whispered. "Yes."

What? Do you want my permission to explore this ... this whatever shit? she recalled Dell asking many moons ago.

Kink, honey.

An open marriage? You want to watch me have sex with other women? I can't watch you...

"You've felt it too," Gavin said, interrupting her daydream as he guided her eyes back to his. "A stab of pain so sharp it nearly rends you in two. Yes?"

She nodded, dropped her gaze.

"Jealousy is a fear of losing something that was never ours to begin with."

She noticed he waited for her to absorb his forthright words.

"I'm. Not. Afraid. Of. Losing. You."

Audrey stared into the starry-night sky of his eyes. Grabbing him at the nape of his neck, she pulled his face closer and kissed him.

"Do you have any idea the pleasure it brings me to fulfill your fantasies and desires? To watch other people touch you. To watch you touch them. It brings me joy witnessing your joy. I feel love watching you love. Some people feel jealousy and compersion at the same time. It's beautiful, Audrey."

"Gavin," she said, the ache she felt in her back and loins somehow present in her voice.

"Have you imagined me with Peyton?"

Audrey's eyes closed in slow motion, and as they reopened, she was positive they were filled with not only lust, but a deep-seated desire to see him experiencing satisfaction through his encounters with another man. No one person could be anybody's everything. Years of marriage had taught her that lesson.

"Yes, sir," she said in a husky voice.

"Audrey, that's compersion."

Gavin brought her back to the here and now — the two of them in his private room, her hands cuffed, a leash attached to them — by kissing her forehead, her cheeks, her lips.

"You're my good girl," he said, his voice like that of a hypnotist ending a session. "You'll remain chained to my bed until it's time for you to go. I'll see to your needs. Do you want anything right now?"

She nodded, leaned forward, rested her forehead against his, and shared his breath.

"Oh, baby girl," he said, sighing with such tenderness, stroking her cheeks, and then they kissed. "What will we do with you? Such innocence and such needs. You'll learn to let go of this shame." He kissed her again, speaking against her mouth, whispering, "I own you. I own your mouth. Your lips. Your body. Your fucking soul."

The kiss grew deeper, more passionate, and as he gave her his tongue — his softer side, or maybe that was his only side, his feelings in the form of nonstop delicious kisses — her body bloomed with newfound emotions.

Her petals opened.

She stood in the sun.

Blooming with love.

And compersion.

20

It was the first time she'd been in the club without access to her phone. The dungeon rules forbade the use of phones/cameras/video in certain areas. She'd always kept it anyway, securing her phone under a bra strap or at the waist of her underwear. Gavin had taken it tonight, though, before he left the room, promising to guard it with his life.

"It won't leave my person," he'd said. "I will check it. I'll respond to your father as though it's you. Let this go, Audrey. You're with me. I take care of your needs."

But she couldn't let it go.

She'd been lying in his bed for what felt like hours, but without a clock or television or computer, without a window, she had no concept of time.

Alone with her thoughts and watching blobs of paint take shape on the ceiling, she could only think of the mistakes she'd made, her regrets — all the ways she could've been a better mom. How she could've been a better wife. A more well-rounded woman.

Was this what Gavin had meant by meditation? Audrey called it torture. And not the good kind.

The silence ate her alive ... until it didn't — until she wouldn't allow it. She rubbed herself almost to the point of sleep. Gavin didn't often disavow her need for self-pleasure or put stipulations on it. In fact, he encouraged it.

Even without a window, she assumed it was late. Gavin hadn't yet returned. And although she knew he hadn't played with others without her present — other than Peyton — she still wondered if he lied or needed more than just her submission to him and his to Peyton.

The things he hid in his eyes haunted her dreams:

His son Michael.

His former submissive who'd taken her life.

An ex-wife.

Years and years of fetishes and kink.

Peyton...

Gavin had never detailed his relationship with Kate's Dominant. Audrey had never asked. But she had imagined. And she wanted to know more ... and then at the same time, she didn't. What if she did feel jealousy? What if it changed things?

Audrey must've finally fallen asleep.

She sucked in a breath the moment she opened her eyes. Gavin lay next to her on his side, facing her, and he was awake, staring at her. His shoulders looked even wider at this angle, his chest hair darker, his stubble filled with more shadow. Everything about him seemed heightened — especially his gaze. His blue eyes burned into her brown ones, starting a fire.

She blinked, trying to focus.

"Good morning," he said, then kissed her nose.

"Mmm, it's morning?" She stretched her cuffed hands above her head as she yawned, and he followed the line of chain and smiled. "I'm hungry."

"Go start the shower. Wait for me under the stream." He

stripped the sheet off her body, then smacked her ass after she stood.

Letting out a little yelp, she gave him a smile as she sauntered to the bathroom, chain dragging on the floor behind her, rattling.

She waited ... and waited ... and then the water turned cold. Despite her teeth chattering and body shivering, she remained under it, adjusting to the temperature.

Cold was only a state of mind.

He finally entered the shower with a cluster of grapes in hand and a smirk in his eyes. Pressing his chest to her back, he fed her until they were gone, then he tossed the stem aside, grabbed her hips, and told her to bend. He fucked her without speaking, only grunting.

The way his nails dug into her skin, the way he would pull out and shove back inside, each thrust more powerful than the last, told her he didn't care if she came, didn't care if she was cold. And she knew all of it made him harder, made him more determined, more dangerous.

And all of it meant she pleased him beyond words.

On one elongated groan, he pulled out and came all over her back. After massaging the warmth of his seed into her skin, he whispered all the words he'd refused to utter moments before as he began to expertly finger her pink hole, caress her seam, and stroke her clit, his chest heaving against her back, his lips nibbling her ear.

"Beautiful, beautiful," he cried. "Come for me. Sing for me."

Her songs of pleasure echoed across the shower. The cold became insignificant. All that mattered were his words horseback riding through her head. His mastery of her.

Sagging in his arms, her knees buckled as she milked his fingers and pulsated over the whole of his hand.

He pulled her upright and soaped the loofa, then began to

wipe every inch of her body, scrubbing at the faint letters still visible on her chest.

After the crisp, cold shower, he uncuffed her and brought her to the counter, propped her up on it, and covered her body in a large, white towel. As he fed her more grapes and towel dried her hair, she remained unusually quiet. The events of the prior night and meditation that followed had rendered her mute. The silence spoke volumes, saying more than she ever could with sounds and letters and inflections.

"Your father texted once," he said, running fingers through her damp, wavy hair.

"What?" she started, joining the moment. "Is everything okay?"

"Yes..." he began, tugging at the towel, "'*Bean.*' It was only a check-in."

Audrey glanced away, fighting a smile. The familiarity didn't make her uncomfortable. It strangely made her tingle — in all the places.

"Look at me, Bean." He pulled her chin to face him.

"Don't call me that," she said with a wide grin.

"Why? I'm a father to you now."

"You're not even ten years older than me. That's just..."

"I care for your needs." He slid a grape into her mouth. A whole bowl of the juicy little globes sat on the counter. "Dress."

As her feet hit the floor, she turned, and the towel fell. She caught him staring at her chest in the mirror. No matter how much he'd scrubbed at the letters, they were still a little visible. Tracing the outline with her fingers, she remembered the extent of time she'd spent in front of the same mirror last night, staring at her body, her folds, her cunt, her chest, the letters — her eyes. *Meditating.* She'd always hated the chestnut brown she'd inherited from her mother. But last night, she'd fallen in love with the color.

It wasn't narcissism.

She wasn't Warren Beatty.

It was confirmation. A treaty. And she'd made it with herself. Gavin's task *had* taught her a lesson.

He flipped her around in an instant and kissed his way up the faded letters from the T to the S, stopping to suckle at her nipples and breasts, latching on like a baby, sucking until she tried to squirm from his arms and scream.

"Let's try to do this like regular people." Bending her backward, he kissed her neck. "How are your wrists?" He kissed the veins and massaged the bruises.

"Fine." She traced the contours of his face.

Already hard again, even after the cold shower, the man positioned her ass on the counter and found his place inside her body in one fluid motion.

"We'll fuck like regular people," he whispered with a strain and then hit her womb and held himself there.

Audrey whimpered between breath-stealing kisses, followed by ones on her face, cheeks, lips, neck, and breasts.

"Touch yourself," he said, watching her fingers beginning to play with her clit. "Don't wait. You need one more before you go home. Before you leave me."

"Don't." She choked back a sob as he drove into her, kissed her, made love to her...

...but they weren't regular people.

They could never be that. She would go home, and he would stay here. Their worlds would never collide. They would only remain an escape. Each world an escape from the other until one star would give out and die, explode into space, lose its light, become matter, and power someone else's life.

She disguised her sorrow inside her release, cried through the orgasm, because then he wouldn't ask questions, then she wouldn't have to explain the mess of emotions rising within her now.

This man couldn't be a father to her children. He couldn't help with homework or stop Bry and Rick's fighting. The dynamic of a family, her fucking family, would change everything they had *here*. A woman eventually nagged and took too far a lead. A man eventually grew complacent. He would lose respect for her because she would lose respect for him. And then he couldn't command and own her. Her reality would kill the submission, leaving his dominance in the wake.

This.

Was.

It.

If she wanted more, she would settle. It was father, husband, and regular lover — or it was *him* and the loneliness she still suffered every weekend. Lonely for her children when with Gavin ... and lonely for Gavin when she was with the boys.

Motherhood took all her stamina.

And Gavin replenished it.

This.

Was.

It.

Who else would beat her and love her and care for the boys? Burn her and cuddle her and chain her to the bed, write slurs on her breasts, make her suck cock after cock after cock, dream of sharing her with two others he loved? Who else would abuse her the way she desired?

Maybe she should settle for regular: black coffee, minivans, a faithful man who came home and gave a damn.

She'd tried that already.

Went to therapy.

Nothing she imagined truly existed.

Except this.

And the fantasies Gavin fulfilled and wanted to fulfill still scared the shit out of her. She had to go home so she could return. Put the collar away — trade it for T-shirts and jeans.

Moments later she emerged from the bathroom, dressed in a pale-pink ribbed sweater, beige pencil skirt, and knee-high suede boots, pressing glittery peach gloss between her lips.

"How did you spend the evening?" he asked, soaking in her ensemble from head to toe.

"How did you spend it?" she deflected.

"Did you touch yourself?"

"We can do this all day, Gav, but I have to go."

"You're still wearing my collar, Audrey." His voice was sliding down the side of a rocky mountain in a thunderstorm. "Answer me."

Placing her palm at her throat, fingering the symbol of his protection and ownership, she smiled weakly. "Yes, I touched myself. I came twice. I went through your drawers. I flipped through your photo album." She nodded toward the shelf. "Looked through some books. I stared in the mirror for hours."

"Meditating."

"Then I fell asleep, hungry and tired and minus the shame you saw on my face when you left me."

"I never leave you." Stalking forward, he clutched her throat. "Always. *Right here*," he said, squeezing. "What did you see in the mirror?"

"A mother with tiny breasts."

Dell had always wanted her to have enhancement surgery (his words, not hers) after Ricki. *God forbid he call it* a *boob job*. Her breasts were A cups. She had no jiggle, only little mounds topped with fucking fantastic (she had to admit) nipples.

"A belly that isn't flat or smooth," she continued. "Wrinkles on my thighs and forehead."

"You saw more than skin," he said, tracing the lines near her temples. "You learned something. I can see it in your eyes."

She would choke. Right. Now. Or maybe she would cough or cry or bleed. Why did he need every part of her? He had her holes. He owned her pleasure. He could humiliate her in front of dozens. Even hundreds. And still ... he wanted her heart. Why? He would only break it.

"The exercise wasn't a waste. You spent the time thinking ... without responsibility or expectation. Only you, your thoughts, ideas, and dreams. No chores. No mouths to feed. No screens to occupy your space. No distraction, Audrey. That's meditation. It scared you. And so, you're lying to me. You focus on the vanity. And you're not vain. Nor are the things you see as imperfections any cause for concern.

"This belly held children." He caressed it for several long seconds. "These breasts fed them." His thumbs stroked her nipples over her sweater. "These eyes"—he touched the lids— "and this face ... reassure boys turning into men — you move mountains."

Bottom lip trembling, she pushed his hands away, but he cradled her face, nuzzled her nose.

"It wasn't wasted," he repeated. "I had to keep myself from you last night, so you could have this. I knew it was the only way for you to obey me in this task." He kissed her open palm. "Go home and then come back to me. Always." He tugged her hair — one, two, three.

Audrey was the first to break their gaze. She grabbed her weekender and purse but paused when she reached the door.

"I love you, Gavin," she said without looking at him.

"Audrey?"

"Yeah." She glanced over her shoulder and met his eyes.

"You make me feel like anything is possible. And the man who used to feel like that ... he died a long time ago."

21

"Where did you get your name?"

Audrey blinked several times at Gavin's request. They lay in bed — his king bed in his private room — facing one another. She must've fallen asleep, unaware of the time, didn't even know if it was day or night. But it wasn't the first time she'd awoken to him staring into what had been her closed eyes.

Now they were open.

"My mom," she said and blinked, swallowed memories. "Are we having pillow talk, Gavin Sellers?" Audrey's lips went from zero to sixty, racing toward a checkered flag of a smile.

He dragged a finger from her temple to her chin. "Did she give you this iridescence too, Audrey Bianca Simone?" His quiet question was coupled with a serious face, heat in his gaze, love strung out amongst his vocal chords.

The memories Audrey had swallowed — her mom's irre-placeable face ... her natural beauty ... the peanut butter cookies she made from scratch ... the way she made people come alive when she read children's stories, becoming any character easily ... the never-ending, squeeze-you-tight hugs — ballooned, not just in her heart, but in her throat, scraping it dry.

"What is it, baby girl?" He wiped near the corner of her eye, painting her skin with salt and affection.

"My mom ... she named me..." Audrey smiled through the tears. "She loved Audrey Hepburn. I think she probably saw *all* of her films. Her favorite was *My Fair Lady*."

Gavin's thumbs were still caressing the creases near her lids when Audrey shifted her eyes. Rubbing her feet in a steady rhythm against his, she attempted in vain to avoid his all-knowing, soul-climbing into-her-soul stare.

"When did she pass?" he asked as though he were God. He'd witnessed life and death and miracles. Their eyes locked.

"How did you know?"

"Because I know my girl. I see your heart. I can feel your pain here." He placed a hand on her chest.

"Bryson was a baby." Her words came out with a sharp sigh. "Ricki wasn't a thought on the horizon. She never met him." Audrey didn't know why she needed to state the obvious. It was just one of those things one said to fill the ugly space death occupied.

"I used to take Michael to classic movies at the theatre here in downtown."

"Yeah?"

"Every summer, they have quite a lineup, one each weekend. Michael learned to appreciate them."

"When did you stop? How long has it been?"

"I lost track." He pulled the covers off her body. "I want to burn you. Turn over."

He stepped away, lit two candles — red and pink, blood and sex, love and survival — and then he came right back and straddled her thighs.

"A burn for each summer he's been out of my life. We'll pour the pain out together. Yes?" he said as he dripped the first lost summer onto her supple, waiting skin.

"Fuck … yes, please."

"Please what?"

"Please, *Master*," she said, exhaling with relief, and he did another. "Please burn your girl tonight." Gasping, she closed her eyes as he dribbled more liquid across her backside, surrendering to the sensational feeling only wax could provide.

"That was three. I never lose track of time, Audrey. Isn't that right?"

"Yes, sir."

He set the candles aside, covered his chest in oil, and then he lay his chest against her back, pressing himself against her. Flesh on flesh. Wax on wax. Blood to love. Pain to redemption.

They would burn together.

Stick together.

Become one in their pain and peel away the layers once it dried.

22

"Come in, Audrey."

Black T-shirt clinging to his body like a second skin, biceps flexing with each subtle but systematic movement, his eyes on the wall in front of him — how had he known she was there? From several feet away, she peeked into the kitchen, watching him perform a task she'd never imagined seeing him orchestrate.

But he did orchestrate it.

And well.

He did this the way he did everything involving the intricate use of his hands.

"How did you know I was there?" She stepped farther into the kitchen. All the countertops were stainless. It had a sink and an oven, a few shelves, and a refrigerator.

"The same way I know when to stop adding water. When to stop playing with the flour and yeast." He placed a piece of the moist dough inside her mouth. "It tells me."

As he looked into her eyes, she was convinced he saw a child. A girl. Someone who needed a man's attention. And in an instant, he snatched the gift of his undivided attention away and focused on kneading.

"You disobeyed me." His biceps flexed with each roll and push.

The sensation in her mouth — the squishy, salty, yeasty piece — had at first been sweet and pungent. Now, it was only sour, leaving an unpleasant aftertaste.

"You don't want me here?" She sounded smaller than she'd hoped. True, he hadn't asked for her yet. She must've been sleeping when he left the room, but she hadn't been bound or tied.

"Don't infer things, Audrey." He shaped. Twisted. Formed. "We have an agreement. If you're in my bed, you're to await my instructions."

"I'm sorry, sir."

Six lumps went into six pans, his strong hands shaping them into good-sized loaves. "We don't bake bread together or break it. We don't hold hands."

But he'd spent eons securing her in his arms, staring into her eyes, and he'd been keeping her overnight. They had said they loved each other many times. Why was he being so cold — in the warm room, next to the warm oven and the lukewarm dough?

Audrey's eyes blurred, fixating on Gavin's fingers, his watch, the oven lights. Then her gaze traveled back to her Master's deft hands while her mind conjured up the feel and smell and taste of another man: Dell Simone. A man who'd always wanted to hold her hand. Well, until their second son had been born. Until one day, holding hands went out to the curb with the trash pickup. Forgotten like nightly dinners at the dining room table.

.   .   .

It was a late summer night many years ago... Dell had driven Audrey to a lake where light pollution was scarce. The promise of a meteor shower began to finally fulfill itself after an hour of patiently waiting.

Several summers had already been spent in the Florida heat after Audrey's father had moved his family to the Sunshine State when she was a teen. However, this was her first June, July, and August spent with Dell.

But at eleven o'clock at night, mosquitoes biting, a tepid wind howling over the water at unexpected intervals, she still hadn't quite gotten used to the temperature change. Her place of birth had been Wilkes-Barre, Pennsylvania.

Sitting next to the cutest guy she knew, at the ripe age of twenty-one, full of dreams and hormones, helped Audrey forget the humidity and the bugs ... almost. The streaks of light making a showcase across the black blanket above were what really erased her silent complaints, though.

"Did you see that one, A?" he asked.

Both of them sat atop his car hood, feet and shins dangling off the edge as they scanned the canopy of blinking lights. The sky's constellations and the ember of Dell's cigarette were the only other lights for miles. Crickets competed with their sparse conversation. The silence they often shared was comforting the way a sleepover could be with your best friend. Knowing both when to gab and when to lie still. When to wax poetic about nothing.

"Dang, I missed it." Her eyes did a quick scan of the heavens. "Oooh. There's one."

They watched it burn, leaving a wormlike trail in a split second. And then, as if on instinct, their eyes met.

Each time Dell took a drag, or whenever he was pensive — and it wasn't brooding; although people mistook it for brooding because he had this "fuck with me, and I'll fuck with you" face —

his eyes crinkled at the corners, extending out toward his temples. He was young, but he crinkled. His smile pronounced the lines. But Dell's smile was often internal. If you knew where to look for it, you could find it.

Audrey knew where to look.

They'd been friends now for months. When they'd met, she'd been dating someone. He'd been dating someone. Now, they were free.

Funny, Audrey wouldn't know the true meaning of that word for at least fourteen more years.

Free to be with each other, but they were still platonic. Dell hadn't made a move. She knew he liked her, though. But first base didn't even seem to be on his radar, not with her anyway. She could tell he fostered pent-up frustration, and she wondered where he went to placate the need.

Audrey went under the covers or in the shower. Her hand was getting a workout, and she wanted to be filled with something other than a toy or her own fingers.

They kept watching the sky, losing track of time. The hands of the clock were the light of another of Dell's cigarettes.

"What are you doing?" she gasped as his hand made contact with her bare thigh.

He'd slapped it hard, and his palm remained flush against her skin. And the touch — the slap, the sting, and the five fingers resting way above her knee and close to her apex of burning fucking heat — had her pussy clenching and face flushing.

"A mosquito," he replied, a real Dell smile on his face, lighting his eyes, pronouncing the crinkles.

"You aren't just trying to get into my pants?" She wiggled, giving him a subtle invitation to move those fingers higher.

"No, sweetheart." He exhaled a cloud of smoke in the other direction as Audrey glanced away. But he squeezed her knee, rousing her attention. "I've been trying to figure out how to go about holding your hand all night."

She took the cigarette from him, smiled, and put it between her lips.

"Is that all it takes?" he asked.

As she inhaled, then coughed, he patted her back while looking like he was trying not to laugh, then he took the filter and flicked it.

Audrey stared down at his hand. The one that had resumed its former position: bending backward, wrist out, fingers — hairless and knuckles pale — splayed toward the windshield. He looked relaxed. Unencumbered.

Audrey touched him.

Not the way she had when she'd stolen his smoke, although their skin had sparked then too. But she touched him with intention. Answering his silly request with the gentle placement of her hand on his. Fingers intertwining. Skin flush against skin. Clammy palms meeting for the first time.

Dell kissed Audrey on top of the hood and under the stars.

And with that first kiss began a union that would last over ten years and result in two beautiful children being born.

The whole summer of being twenty-one and in love passed with kisses — fevered, passionate, tongue-mingling-with-tongue kisses. June, July, and August passed ... and he waited.

Holding her hand every time they were together — movies, stargazing, the beach — and he waited. Dry humping became a sport. Mutual masturbation sessions the medal. Penetration the goal.

But he waited...

And now, she was here.

In a kitchen with Gavin.

At the far end of a very different spectrum, and she wanted the code to unlock the secret door.

Always a locked door to a man's heart.

Audrey had wondered that first summer...

How do I get Dell to fuck me? Take me? Pin me? Bite me? Lead me? Stop treating me like a delicacy?

And now she wondered...

How do I get Gavin to hold my hand? Allow me to touch him when I want to? How do I get him to visit my home? How do I reach this other part of him?

What if that part didn't exist? Though she'd seen it in action several times, in his eyes constantly.

What if he didn't need the other part?

What if she didn't need it from him either?

Then why was there cotton in her mouth and throat? Why couldn't she swallow?

Would certain pieces of a man ever be enough? Why was wanting everything from a single person — an improbability — a necessity, an obsession, the end goal?

Dell had always been too much of a gentleman to take advantage of Audrey's willingness in the early days. Hell, even during their marriage, Dell had sometimes treated her like a princess — an out-of-reach goddess.

Audrey knew now why the whorehouse had been invented.

Men had desires that needed to be satisfied, but they placed their wives high up on princess' pedestals where they wouldn't be bothered with things like masculine urges, fetishes, and demands. Horny men were blind to the fact that their wives might have similar urges.

Forbidden ones. Dirty ones.

And then there was another beast. A different kind of animal altogether: men who had their heads so far in the sand they didn't even know what they wanted or desired. They denied that they fantasized. The possibility of fetish or play outside the box of how a man — a gentleman — *should behave* with their lover/wife/girlfriend was buried in two hundred feet of Freudian/religious/parental muck.

Audrey may have at one time been one of those suppressed ostriches.

Now, she was an owl and an eagle. A student who knew precisely what she wanted and who she wanted for a teacher. What she needed scared the shit out of her because knowing didn't mean the ideal existed or that she could have it. Knowing meant choosing. And she'd already chosen to let go of one good man.

Dell...

Love had died. Withered.

And this man, Gavin Sellers, her Master whom she loved — a love that people, civilization, and this modern world we call *advanced intelligent society* would say was anything but — couldn't break role. Gavin was Daniel Day Lewis in *Lincoln*. Val Kilmer in *The Doors*.

Call me Jim.

Call me Mr. President.

Can't break role.

It wasn't love. It was an addiction. A want. Hedonism. Love wasn't supposed to look like Gavin and Audrey.

Black and blue. Collar and chain. Hands tied. Nipples clamped. Ass and thighs covered with glorious welts and abstract bruises. Holes raw and sore and begging. Jaw aching. Voyeurism and sharing. No entanglements. No family tree branches dangling. No dating or movies. No "normalcy."

No bread making or breaking.

No handholding.

Heart made of glass and complete with a little hammer ready to shatter the illusion...

That...

...was Gavin and Audrey.

Love looked like Cinderella and Prince Charming. Julia Roberts and Richard Gere. Love even looked like Nicolas Cage and Cher.

But Gavin and Audrey?

Fuck... Audrey thought as he slid two loaves of bread in the oven. *I love him. I physically ache for him. Emotionally and spiritually too.*

He placed two more pans on the wire rack as her mind continued its journey to the foregone conclusion she'd been denying for weeks...

Nights I'm away and in my bed alone ... at the dinner table where the fourth chair sits empty ... during car rides to Disney... Fuck... I want my boys to meet him.

Fuck. Fuck. Fuck.

Life wasn't some stupid fucking Hollywood movie. And if it was, hers wouldn't have been fairy-tale-bullshit princess dreams. The title of her movie would've been more akin to *Looking for Mr. Goodbar,* only without the abhorrent ending.

"Wait for me in my room, Audrey," he said without turning around or acknowledging her, his dominant voice a line drive to both her heart and pussy. "In position."

His cadence spoke volumes, informing her he'd already seen the memories of past relationships glazing over the brown of her eyes, turning their chestnut into dark chocolate.

But he couldn't read her thoughts.

Except ... he could.

Audrey had no doubt she'd be in Gavin's room, knees on the floor, palms up, spread open, for as long as he wished to keep her there. Waiting for a man she craved and loved and feared — who had no intention of ever holding her hand — to punish her, fuck her, chain her, push her, dominate, and humiliate her ... do all the things she thought a family man couldn't provide.

It was tit for tat.

This or that.

She chose Gavin fucking Sellers.

23

Weekends weren't always filled with excess and the goings-on of the dungeon. Some nights included meet-ups or classes, conversations and wine — separate from the atmosphere at Bodhi. Some Sunday mornings were spent talking to Darcy. The woman came in early once a month on Sunday, usually to take inventory.

"What else do you like to do, Darc?" Audrey popped an olive into her mouth.

"You mean besides this glamorous job?"

"Yeah."

Darcy put her elbows on the counter, then pushed on the bridge of her large, square-rimmed glasses. "I just opened up a tattoo parlor."

"No shit."

"Do you have one?"

"No, I don't have a parlor."

"Brat." Darcy stuck out her tongue.

Audrey laughed. "No, I don't have a tat."

"Want one? I can hook you up, kid."

"Maybe. I've thought about it. I have no idea what I want, though. Gavin has been giving me ideas."

"I'm sure he has." Darcy bounced her eyebrows. "He'd probably love to carve a penis on your forehead."

"Stop." Audrey clutched her stomach, laughing.

"And what do you do ... away from all this kinky shit?" Darcy blinked. "Wait." She put a palm in the air. "Let me guess."

Audrey put her elbows on the counter too, mimicking Darcy. Although no one could imitate Darcy. She was a one-of-a-kind loveable bitch.

"Okay ... you're an elementary school teacher."

"Nope."

"Social worker?"

"Nope."

"Hmmm..." Darcy tapped a hot-pink acrylic nail against her cheek.

"Open your mouth." Audrey smiled.

"What? You wanna see my tongue ring?" Darcy opened and said, "*Ahhh.*"

Audrey winced at the sight of the bar spliced between the muscle. "No. Show me your teeth." Unable to help herself, Audrey inspected them. "Thank you. You have beautiful teeth."

"Of course I do." Darcy winked and returned to shuffling some boxes around. "You a dentist or something?"

"Or something. I'm a dental assistant."

"That's even more glamorous than what I do here."

"Tell me about it."

"Tell you what?" Gavin said after entering the room.

Audrey jumped. "How do you always do that?"

"You never told me our new little miss kinkster is a dentist."

"Dental assistant."

"You never asked."

"Maybe what you should concern yourself with, Gav, are the things I tell Audrey about *you* when you're not around."

"I am always around. I'm omni."

"Right. I forgot." Darcy snorted.

"How long have you two known each other?"

Gavin's face became somber. Audrey assumed he was thinking of the woman he'd loved, the one who'd committed suicide. Darcy met Gavin's eyes, and they shared one of those telepathic, secret-agent gazes.

"Why don't you take the day off?"

"I'll fall behind."

"Do I have to spell it out?"

"No, sir."

Darcy packed up a few things. "I've known him for sixteen years." She shot Gavin a pointed stare even though she'd spoken to Audrey. "Sometimes he's a real dick."

Audrey couldn't disagree. Most everyone could be a real dick from time to time. But she loved that dick — and the dick's dick. And she was glad they'd be alone for a few hours longer. Her and the dick and the dick's dick.

"When is Kate picking you up?" he asked.

Kate was probably at Peyton's apartment. They played there too. Kate even said they did couple things. Went to the zoo. Ate meals at restaurants. Things Gavin wouldn't dare do. Not with Audrey — a woman who had children, baggage, fears. A woman who wore his collar but couldn't fully commit to the lifestyle.

"Around four."

"Come. I want to show you something." After waiting for Audrey to stand, he placed his hand on the small of her back and guided her to his private room.

His laptop was open, and he clicked on a folder entitled *Blog Drafts*. Audrey's eyes were riveted to the screen. Her breath caught. She had to remind herself to release the air from her lungs.

"Sit," he commanded, then began to braid her hair.

Audrey bathed in this simple act of care — it never ceased to get old. Once finished, he placed one hand flat on the desk and the other on the touch pad — his biceps were practically grazing her face — as he clicked open a specific document.

"Read these two." He bent lower and kissed her neck. "I want to share the ugly parts of myself with you."

"Nothing..." She swallowed. "No parts of you are ugly."

"Audrey, I've had to find my own version of God."

She blinked the way the cursor did, her eyes on the unpublished essays.

"Stay here until I come for you. When you finish reading, be in position."

Turning her head toward him, she whispered with no inhibition, "Yes, sir," then proceeded to read the inner chamber of her Master's heart.

The two essays were untitled.

She wondered if they had no beginning and no end.

———

The first time I asphyxiated Harper, I felt a metaphysical calm, something other-worldly which radiated beyond the neurological pathways leading to my mind. The sensations traveled outside my nervous system. Outside my body.

I could describe this calm in several different ways. But the best way — the memory that grips my heart with an iron fist at unsuspecting times during the day or night — was the minute Michael was born.

Practicing breath play gave me a calm I hadn't felt since I'd held my child for the first time — the little boy who became a man and no longer wished to own the title "son."

My son.

Strange in a way.

Not that he refuses to call me dad or father or anything at all for that matter. But strange because on the day of his birth, I felt a palm-grazing-the-tops-of-the-wheat-field peace in a moment when many first-time parents might've experienced both serenity *and* panic.

Strange ... because the peace both of those experiences provided was similar in nature.

The way Harper's eyes fluttered open, then closed, and the way her breath slowed when I held my palm to her neck. The way she trusted me implicitly to care for her — the way my son also did at one time — was something I never took for granted.

She had beautiful eyes even when closed. Shaped not like almonds — a cliché — and not sloped like the doe-eyed Audrey Hepburn, but round and soft and inquisitive. Beautiful. Like an angel had christened her pupils, the irises, the everything that went into making them majestic. The wings of a cherub had painted God's beauty on the pale of her skin and in the deep chasms of her blue eyes.

My hand on her throat ... I'd float watching her lashes flutter.

My name would pass her lips on the way out of consciousness and again on the way back in.

I could bring her back to life.

I thought I was her redeemer.

Her savior.

Her Jesus fucking Christ.

Until the day arrived when I wished to stop believing any *fishers of men* existed.

No one could save her.

Not Christ.

Certainly not me.

She had hung...

...lifeless.

Without support.

In the end, she had no one.

And that's why Bodhi exists. Because Harper convinced me to open this sanctuary. Because she'd needed exactly that.

A place to be normal again in a world full of self-righteous do-gooders.

I built this house of worship, and I lost a son.

Another Son provided redemption.

I lost a girl with angel-kissed eyes.

But I'd gained a tribe.

———

After Harper died. I died. I found it increasingly difficult to participate in the kink I taught and craved.

Peyton brought me back to life.

I started referring to my past as Before Peyton. It eased my mind. Made me think I was changing or I could change. Except ... I didn't believe in metamorphosis, not the way most people teach it. Religion teaches change. Correction: religion teaches the guise of change. Follow the Law to the letter, and you'll be a better man.

Stop drinking.

Abstain from sex.

Don't lie or steal or cheat.

And people pay out the nose to risk believing in it. And their hearts pay too — they break. Their souls pay because they can no longer be redeemed. Hope is taken from them when they no longer accept traditions, and they're left to find their own paths. They must learn the hard way...

People can stop doing certain things: proclivities, activities, habits.

But people don't change.

Desire remains potent and alive, never having left them or me or us. Eating away at willpower. And Before Peyton, I would lie in bed after an evening spent brutalizing another human being in all the ways they'd begged me to — their marked skin an imprint on my soul — and I'd ponder everything religion hadn't taught me.

I ended up with a long list of nagging doubts and questions.

Not being able to change wasn't an excuse to misbehave. It wasn't a license to sin. But it was a key to unlocking a mystery.

A mystery named fear.

And religion did a fine job cultivating, then helping me maintain, the fears I harbored ... fear after fear after fear.

Michael thrived on it. Lots of people do, whether they're aware of it or not. Fear keeps them in line. It gives them hope.

I sought freedom from that form of slavery. And I harnessed the momentum I felt in discovering this new-found religion, and I shed the chains of the old rites and became the man God meant for me to be.

The precise, choreographed, deliberate ministrations I learned, then executed — the innate need for control I finally embraced — led me to the true path of inner peace...

Bodhi.

Yet ... the girl I loved was never far from my mind. And Peyton's exorcisms couldn't ever take her away. Nor were they supposed to.

Each time I pressed my thumb to her neck, each time her knees gave way and I kept her intact ... each time I pushed a first, second, and then a third finger into her tight ring of muscle, and finally my dick — because her ass was mine ... each scream, gasp, breath ... each sigh — rendered me in absolute fucking control. And no nighttime regimen of thinking about sons and sin and metamorphosis could take that away.

The dungeon we built would be forever.

Black and blue, the tattoo I offered.

And twisted, beaten, pinched, suffocating — beautiful — skin would be the daily sacrifice I would feast on.

24

sometimes when he fucks me
    a thumb presses into the hollow of my neck
    not lightly
    held there
    pressing
    with a push into the skin
    how far can he go does he wanna go
    He Pushes It Deeper
    He Squeezes Tighter
    gripping my neck with his fingers
    darkness dancing in his eyes
    that I've never seen
    sometimes I'm afraid of his eyes ... and the look in them
    yet
    he cannot discern his gaze or interpret it
    whenever I'm beneath him
    owned
    used
    held
    and his hand circles my neck

his thumb in the hollow
it belongs, belongs, belongs
his eyes alight with mirth and death
the semblances mixing together
until the opposing forces unite
becoming one and the same

25

The four of them had already walked the square in its entirety but had been unable to sample every vendor at the Saturday Morning Market. The early February air still had a bite, the steady wind blowing across the Bay feeding the tents its breeze. Music played from a traveling vendor — a man at a large keyboard. CDs for sale and a box for donations were set up near the front and off to the side.

Audrey fished for some cash in her wallet while squinting at a nearby white canopy opposite her when her body gave way.

With the money in her fist and what was sure to be a deer-caught-in-the-headlights look in her eyes, she almost tipped to the side. But her knees locked, and she righted herself as she looked away from the sharp Copenhagen gaze of the man who held her heart in his stare.

Clearing her throat, she spoke to Rick, handing him the ten. "Buddy, go put this money in the box."

"Can I have a CD?"

"Sure."

Audrey could feel Gavin's starry sky burning a hole through

her skin. Kate and Bryson were busy watching the piano man when her phone buzzed in the palm of her hand.

Gavin: Do you have on the panties I told you to wear?

Audrey bit her lower lip, glanced at him, but he was now busy speaking to a customer. She nudged Kate, then nodded in Gavin's direction.

"You knew he would be here?" Audrey whispered, unsure whether she was mad or scared or tingly. Maybe all three. Lines were blurring, and she hadn't moved a foot since spotting him.

Kate shrugged, keeping her eyes on the musician. Audrey didn't miss her friend's wicked smile. She dragged her focus back to the screen. His question was inappropriate. Right?

They were at a market in St. Pete. She was with her boys. But then Audrey realized if she continued this line of thinking, she would become a self-fulfilled prophecy.

Audrey's job was to please her Master. Not nag him. Not doubt him. She needed to respond as she would naturally.

Gavin: You're hesitating.

Audrey: Yes, sir. I'm wearing them.

Gavin: Good girl.

Audrey chewed on a fingernail. Gavin had retreated to the rear of the tent, his vision on the phone or the woman working at his side. Never on Audrey. And still, he owned her no matter where he was or what he was doing, those damn blue eyes guiding her path.

The musician finished, people clapped, and then he addressed Rick into the microphone. "What song would you like to hear, young man?"

Audrey nodded. "Go on, baby, pick a song."

"Go talk to him," Kate said as Ricki made his way to the singer's table.

"Talk to who?" Bryson looked around.

"No one, Bry," Audrey said, and her son rolled his eyes.

Gavin: You want to ask me questions?

Audrey: Yes.

She glanced at Gavin, trying to hide her smile from Bryson.

Gavin: They're more than I could've imagined.

Their eyes met. She fought tears. He looked away and appeared to be typing.

Gavin: I donate my bread here.

Audrey looked up at the sign.

Bread for Wonder Women.
All profits benefit the St. Petersburg Women's Shelter and The Center
for Victims of Domestic Violence.

Audrey noticed Bryson had followed her eyeline, and her son stared at Gavin, squinting.

Gavin: Come to me.

Hands shaking, Audrey slid her phone into her purse. Again, her inclination was to deny him. Maybe real life squashed the submission she'd promised him just as she'd predicted it might.

Gavin knew her too well. He would sense her hesitation. He would know she was a poser. A little girl who could only play at Bodhi. She wanted him in her life, yet if she couldn't prove she could maintain the dynamic even in the face of "reality," what hope would they have of ever being partners outside the dungeon? Would she ever brave wearing his collar 24/7?

Her neck felt bare.

"Jesus, Audr," Kate said, "your cheeks." She placed the back of her hand against Audrey's heated face. "Go." Kate nodded. "I'll take the boys around a bit. Text me."

"Bry. Rick. I'll be back in a few minutes. Stay with Katy."

"He hasn't finished the song," Rick said.

Bryson's eyes — still narrowed and intense — were on Gavin's biceps.

"Auntie Kate will get you some kettle corn."

Audrey grabbed Bryson's shoulders and met her son's pensive green eyes. He was beginning to look more and more like his father. Kate and Rick stood a few feet away, listening to the man singing Rick's selection. One of Dell's favorites. "Yesterday".

"He's my friend," Audrey said only to Bryson on an exhale.

"The one you see in Tampa?"

"Yes, buddy." Young and pensive and intuitive.

"Why haven't we met him?"

"It's—"

"Complicated," Bryson interjected, rolling those eyes again.

Audrey smiled at her son while imagining another kind of Saturday morning...

Hand in hand with Gavin, the boys beside them, frustrated at accepting a man into her life but trying and adapting. Gavin holding her submission in the palm of his hand. A Master in every sense of the word.

No doubting. Only trusting. No anxiety. Only hope.

The four of them strolling the market. A normal day with normal people. But the breeze would tickle her partially bare cunt, reminding her she would obey him in all things — and the anticipation of how he'd bind her and gag her later that night in their home would light a fire in her mind, burning through the ordinary trees, singeing the vanilla leaves.

Audrey was his.

He was hers.

The boys would come around.

She would wear the necklace proudly.

Two worlds would not only collide — they'd blend.

26

"I don't know if you're a badass or a pain in the ass," Darcy said as she winked. Today, Darcy's hair had green streaks through the blonde. She'd had this color for at least two weeks. A record.

Audrey would drink to Darcy's wild consistency.

"Just provide the glass, please. And the key."

Audrey swung her feet from the seat while holding the neck of the bottle — a pinot noir she'd brought from the outside she had decided to open here. She didn't care if it was only two in the afternoon. Darcy said Gavin had gone out and hadn't said when he'd return. The two-drink maximum wouldn't apply to her this afternoon because the wine was *hers*. Except, she wore the necklace, the collar, the symbol declaring to their world that she did as he wished — and she knew he wouldn't wish for this.

And for that reason alone, she would drink. She would drink for reasons she couldn't ascertain.

"Will you join me, Darc?" Audrey asked while raising the full glass of red in the air.

"No, love. I don't drink."

"Never?"

"Nope."

"Why does he keep the bar?"

"It came with the place." She shrugged. "He likes the look of the thing. It's part of the character."

So much underappreciated liquor. People were too busy getting stoned on bruises and burns. They didn't need alcohol with a place catering to freedom, arousal, and anticipation.

Laughter interrupted the girls' conversation. Manly laughter. Loud and deep and full of mischievous wonder. *The two of them must've come in another door.*

Darcy buried her face in her laptop at the other end of the bar as Audrey took her time entertaining the bottle of red. The vanilla and spice and cherry flavors slid through her veins like lava coursing its way down a mountain. She enjoyed the burn.

She tried to tell herself she'd just been really thirsty as she finished off her fourth and final glass ... and where were those happy, laughing men?

She'd "spoken" too soon.

The two of them, both in tight shirts, Peyton in shorts, Gavin in dark jeans, were heading down the hallway. Once Peyton caught her eye, he smirked then retreated the way he'd come. Gavin, however, didn't pull out from anything. He continued to walk toward the bar, his feet bare, his expression unyielding.

His face told her what she needed to know: she'd displeased him.

She'd come to Bodhi on a whim and without telling him. An absolute no-no. And she'd drunk an entire fucking bottle of wine. Today, she wasn't feeling very submissive. She was feeling testy — tired of playing games and not enjoying the other parts of an adult relationship.

"I wanted to surprise you," Audrey said, planting an elbow on the counter and her chin in her palm, her other hand fingered the collar. She smiled through the hazy glow of her buzz, relishing it before he killed it.

Gavin glanced at Darc, then at Audrey, then he shook the bottle.

"Uh, uh, uh," Audrey said, grinning like a cat full of lascivious cream. "That's mine." She tapped the side with her fingernail. "I drank it ... *all.*"

"Darcy," Gavin barked.

"She brought it with her, sir."

Audrey covered her mouth and let out a tiny squeak.

"Fuck me," Gavin hissed, palms splayed on the counter, head dropped between his shoulders.

Walking her fingers up her favorite biceps, Audrey hiccupped and said, "I'd love to."

Jerking his face toward Audrey, he scowled, lifted her from her seat, and threw her over his shoulder. He smacked her ass and told her to be quiet, and then he shook his index finger at Darcy and gave her orders too.

"She can never drink like this again. In fact, she can't drink."

Fucking asshole is what he is, she thought, her head bouncing, her legs dangling, her stomach contents gurgling as he carried her through the gym and into his studio and dropped her on the bed.

"What's that smell?" Audrey asked, overexaggerating her nostrils and sniffing the air. "Were you burning incense?"

Don't ask Gavin questions... Darcy had always said. Too late. The alcohol made it impossible for Audrey to control her tongue. Maybe the laughter and the smells were part of his *Peyton* secrets. One of the puzzle pieces he left on the floor.

"Take off your jeans," he commanded.

Audrey looked around. The room wasn't so much messy as it was tattered, a little more disheveled than she'd ever seen before. The sheets were rumpled. Did he think he could just bring her in here and she wouldn't ask questions?

"Darcy said you were out."

"I was. Take off your fucking jeans right the fuck now."

She stood and wiggled out of them.

"You know I forbid pants here."

He twisted her body around until her shins hit the bedframe. He caught her fall, but shoved her down anyway, pushing her face into the mattress, holding her neck by the loop on the back of her collar. Then he swatted her ass hard.

"You're not a brat. You're defying me. Why?"

Fuck... He hit her again and again and again. Maybe ten times. Maybe twenty. With a faultless rhythm. A fantastic motion.

She breathed through each strike. The combination of alcohol and pain finally made sense. It was dangerous. Deadly. Because she could take so much more, wanted so much more. And she couldn't go home in the worst fucking shape of her life.

Trailing a finger up her crack, he then circled it over the stinging sensations he'd gifted her ass. "Why did you come here without telling me? Wear jeans and drink an entire bottle of wine?"

"Why are you burning incense? Tell me, who does the pitching? You or him?"

"Do you really think you're ready to know things about me?" he asked with an edge to his voice as he squeezed her cheeks, clawing at the tender skin ... until she wiggled and squirmed and bit back sobs from her throat.

"Yes," she choked out.

He ripped the chalk of his nails across the fleshy blackboard of her ass, causing her to scream. He raked them forward, back and forth until he broke her wide open.

"Stop!" she cried and sniffled. "Stop!"

"Say *king* and it ends, but then I won't let you see more of my story. Say *king*, baby girl. So precious," he said with an ache, swirling his fingertips over her again, coming close to her cunt but never touching it. His hands either swords or plowshares, spears or pruninghooks.

She smacked the bed with a fist. "Do you fuck him?"

"I can fuck whomever I please," he whispered into her ear. "But you know I'm only fucking you. I'm only inside your cunt. Your ass." Each word was a taunt. His voice hissed. She could no longer tell truth from lies. "If you don't trust me, we can't play. If you disobeyed me today because you decided this is not the life for you..."

"Gavin, I—"

"You'll take everything I give you. Stand and face the wall."

The flogger hit her back. It was almost a relief to feel nerve endings come alive in a different location. She sighed. The leather tickled her skin as he alternated between swatting then stroking her with the strands.

"Please," she begged.

Gavin didn't reply with words. He continued to strike her skin until he must've created marks.

"Sir ... please ... tell ... me." Her voice and lips and thighs trembled as each word fell between the lashes.

"You know Peyton dominates me."

Her eyes closed. She saw images flash behind her lids. She swallowed the lump that had taken up residency in her throat. She did know Peyton dominated him. But Gavin had once said he wasn't a switch. Yet, she'd seen the marks and bruises.

There was more between them.

"You will watch."

"No."

"The alcohol does make you bold, Audrey. We will play now, and you aren't supposed to be here, so you'll watch."

"I'll go home."

"You're in my collar. You'll safe out to go home. It's not weak to say your word. I push you on purpose, Audrey, but the trust works both ways. I trust you to use the word when you really need to."

"You ... you won't give me another choice?"

He shook his head. "It's time you see who I am. Fully."

Moments later, Audrey lay handcuffed to the bed, blind-folded, while Gavin prepared the room. She could hear him milling about. Smelled matches. Heard drawers opening and closing.

After what felt like hours, Gavin removed the blindfold, undid her binds, braided her hair, and instructed her to wait on the bed.

Candles filled the room, alight atop the dresser, the desk, the bathroom counter, the nightstand. Every surface was covered with a variety of shapes and sizes and colors. Incense burned too, from somewhere she couldn't ascertain, as though it came from heaven itself.

The shadows climbing the walls from the glow were as intimidating as the two men themselves.

Two. Men.

Peyton had entered and stood only a few feet away, dressed in a dark-brown cloak with a hood covering his sun-kissed locks.

Audrey's stomach shrank to the size of a raisin, but she couldn't speak. Earlier, when Gavin had cuffed her, he'd asked her not to. Demanded her silence. This was his scene, and she was a spectator. He'd told her she should feel privileged to have received the invitation. Because others knew or suspected but they'd never witnessed it. They didn't know the extent of his kinks or fetishes. Only Peyton, Kate, and now Audrey.

"In your position, Audrey," Gavin said, and then he seemed ready to take his own.

She kneeled on the painted concrete floor a few feet from the two men. At no time was she to move unless instructed, unless given a direct command, or she used her safe word. Her skin would tingle, her limbs would turn numb, before she disobeyed him.

Peyton raised two fingers, apparently indicating Gavin obey some preconceived order. Kneeling with one foot on the floor and one knee bent, Gavin bowed his head as Peyton touched his forehead, then his cheeks.

"You wish to have your slave with us tonight?" Peyton asked. Gavin only nodded, keeping his head bowed. "I won't touch her unless you tell me to. Understood?"

Gavin nodded again.

Audrey thought her heart might burst. The two of them shared a heady dominance even when Gavin kneeled. She *had* imagined them together but still sometimes denied it. Still, she had no expectations. Everything here, in this building, in this extravagant world of kink, always surprised her.

People on the outside might've said what was done at the dungeon didn't constitute "normal," but what they failed to realize was that whatever anyone did here was automatically normal once done.

Actually, Gavin hadn't denied being a switch. He'd skirted the question and said he couldn't be defined. Darcy was the one who'd labeled him. It didn't matter. All Audrey wondered was ...

...what were the two of them going to do?

After stroking Gavin's head, Peyton fed him a wafer — *the Eucharist?* — and a sip of what looked like red wine. The men stared into each other's eyes as Peyton whispered blessings and praise. Then he slipped off his hood, untied and removed his robe, ready to begin the rest of what was to follow.

"Show her what I offer to you." Peyton peered down at Gavin. "Show her what you suck and take up the ass."

Audrey inhaled sharply, and Peyton silenced her with a look. She had to concentrate to steady herself. Her knees had begun to wobble. Her chest ached. The scene was something she felt she should stop or participate in or only continue watching. It was a car wreck on the side of the highway.

Who was she?

The doctor or the victim or the passerby?

Her Master's eyes were in a trance. Audrey fought the urge to clap a hand over her mouth and stifled a gasp as the men's eyes locked again, profoundly seeking something from each other she knew she couldn't provide.

Peyton held the base of his shaft as an offering and said, "Make me hard," as Gavin readily took it.

Peyton's head fell back as Gavin began to pump his friend and redeemer. Gavin gripped him, stroked him for an excruciatingly long time, and then, without warning, Peyton put a hand on Gavin's shoulder, and cried, "Stop."

Gavin sat back on his heels, licked his lips, and gazed up at Peyton — lean and long and completely naked, his sunset-burned highlights framing his face and touching his shoulders — seeming to wait for another command. Peyton cupped Gavin's chin as he stared at Audrey, but Gavin wouldn't follow his friend's eyeline. Audrey knew he wouldn't move unless ordered.

Grabbing ahold of the back of Gavin's neck, Peyton thrust into his mouth and fucked him with a force Audrey felt in her loins, but there was no gagging, no retching as he slid in, then out, while caressing Gavin's face.

"*So, so good,*" Peyton said with an ache. "Sucking me off like a good little slave."

The two men enjoyed themselves as though Audrey weren't present. Or maybe they enjoyed themselves more because of it. Gavin looked younger than his forty-one years, his mouth full of a man's cock, his grunting a turn-on, his body a vessel, his fears and grief disappearing and sliding off his skin into a puddle on the floor.

Audrey had no doubt what Gavin felt: the spiritual entanglement, the enlightenment here and now during what might've appeared to be an act of depravity to others.

"You please me," Peyton said, his hand still possessing Gavin's neck, holding his face to his groin. "You please me, Rabboni."

After shoving his cock into her Master's mouth a few more times, Peyton pulled out, put a heel on Gavin's back, and pushed him to the floor. He circled Gavin several times, tapping the tips of his toes to Gavin's body as he did, inspecting him like he was only a piece of meat, making him wait for the next command.

"Pants off. Remove your shirt. Lean over the foot of the bed, facedown, and present yourself to us."

When Peyton returned with a cane, Audrey winced, but Peyton smirked. "Count, slave."

"One, two..." Gavin began as Audrey breathed through the lashes, feeling each strike as though her own. "...thirteen."

"Do you know what thirteen symbolizes in the Bible?" Peyton looked at Audrey. She looked at Gavin.

"Answer me, Audrey."

"My Master told me not to speak."

"Gavin," he said, kicking his legs further apart. The stripes were so red, they appeared raw and bleeding. "Some people think it represents rebellion and lawlessness. Tell her what you think."

Peyton lubed Gavin's hole while he spoke. Audrey began to croak.

"Mysticism is condemned by God," Gavin said as tears filled Audrey's eyes.

But wasn't sodomy condemned too?

"Why the number then?" Peyton asked, the pleasure of what was about to happen apparent in his voice.

"It's always thirteen," Gavin replied.

Peyton dropped to his knees, bored his eyes into Audrey's, and mouthed the word *stop*. Only she could see his lips move.

Then she realized ... *Peyton broke scene.*

It was a scene.

Shhh...

She needed to pull herself together.

A scene. A scene. A scene. Still, her Master — *Rabboni?* — was about to be fucked in the ass by another man, another Dominant, by a friend.

By a man he loved...

Oh God, it was all too much.

Trust, Peyton mouthed and gave her a signal — his hand splicing through the air. *Stop*, he mouthed again. She knew she must've looked a wreck, fearful. Her thighs were quaking, and her bottom lip was being gnawed off by her teeth.

"On all fours," he said, indicating the floor, and Gavin obeyed.

Peyton entered him in one single movement, and she heard Gavin grunt, saw his head drop, but she couldn't see his eyes, nor Peyton's now.

"What's thirteen, Gavin?" Peyton asked on a thrust. "Explain."

Gavin grunted louder. Peyton drove in, then pulled all the way out. Drove in again.

"Tell us."

"It's a blessing," Gavin blurted as his breath shook. Peyton pulled out. He drove in. "A promise." He sounded both pained and fulfilled, complete.

"Audrey," he continued, his voice breaking on the syllables in her name, and then she cried too, quietly, a hand over her mouth, tears falling. "We take what the world calls ugly and defiled and make it beautiful and righteous."

Peyton grabbed his friend's hips and fucked him without

courtesy. Rougher than Audrey had ever witnessed between two men firsthand. Gavin braced himself, a palm on the wall, meeting the pain and the blessing and the promise with his own backward thrusts.

Several minutes later, sweat dripping off Peyton, he grunted his release into Gavin, then collapsed against him. After waiting a moment in silence, both men slumped forward and heaved. Peyton rolled Gavin onto his back.

Audrey could see Gavin's eyes now. They were wide, full of haze, and ready to be climbed into. His starry sky pulled her closer to his heavens even though she remained glued to the floor, her knees spread, tears falling and pussy throbbing.

"Watch her," Peyton growled as he stroked Gavin's cock. Fast, then faster, then even faster. "Watch your little slave."

Gavin's eyes filled with tears. Both Audrey and Gavin cried and choked, and then Gavin came in spurts, his head falling back toward the ground, as he openly sobbed.

Peyton wiped Gavin's forehead, quieted him, reminded him they were safe, then he commanded Audrey to come to them.

"Lick his seed off his body," Peyton said and then went into the bathroom.

Audrey cleaned every inch of Gavin's stomach, inside his belly button and across the hairs of his chest as her tears fell onto his skin. And she licked those too while he fingered her braid, saying nothing.

Peyton returned with water, both to offer drink and to wash. He wiped them both. Audrey's face, her mouth and cheeks, under her eyes. Gavin's chest, face, then his back. Then the two of them, Audrey and Peyton, shared in the job of applying compresses to Gavin's backside and then cream.

The salve had barely dried before Gavin rose, positioned Audrey near the foot of the bed and on Peyton's lap, and began to fuck her with a vigor she feared and craved. Peyton held her backside against his chest and spread her open because he could and because Gavin had given him permission to touch his "little slave." Peyton held her wrists behind her back and one of her thighs out while they watched Gavin regain every bit of strength he'd surrendered.

It was starting to burn. Her cunt. Her eyes. Lines were so blurred she thought maybe they'd never been invented.

"You fucking animal," Peyton hissed, and Audrey imagined the men's eyes meeting in some sort of deep understanding. "You own her." Peyton urged Gavin on when Audrey knew he needed no encouragement. "You fucking own her cunt." Peyton spoke as though he were doing the fucking while he rubbed Audrey's clit, making her involuntarily come while Gavin kept on driving inside her without stopping. As sweat dripped from Gavin's forehead, Peyton smeared it over Audrey's chest, applied kisses to her neck, nibbled her skin.

"You don't even know how alive you are right now." Peyton's voice cracked.

Audrey was certain their eyes remained lock. Gavin's gaze was like a laser beam, blue and wet, and it wasn't on her browns.

"I want her. This," Peyton continued. "All four of us, man."

Audrey couldn't speak. Even though she was the center of all they did, it was as though they didn't need her there, but they did.

"Make her come again," Gavin growled, barely breaking his rhythm. "*Feel. Us. Together.* Touch her cunt and my dick."

Audrey cried out when Peyton went to work again on her clit, massaging it until it burned and burned and burned, and she screamed as he squished a finger into her body alongside Gavin's dick.

Alternating between panting and moaning, she came so hard around Gavin's cock and Peyton's finger it seemed Gavin could no longer hold back his own orgasm.

The second he pulled out, Gavin spilled across her folds, her clit, her hole, her lower stomach, and then Peyton rubbed the semen over her skin, slid his fingers toward her seam, and slipped three fingers inside her warmth, finger fucking her while the two men's eyes met over her shoulder in a fog of lust.

But the third orgasm wouldn't build. She had nothing left. Her heart had cracked open.

She'd finally broken.

"No, no, no ... *king*," she said, wrenching herself from their grasp. "King!" she screamed, and Peyton removed his fingers.

Audrey took off to the bathroom and started the shower, and even though the hot water scalded her, she shook uncontrollably as though she were freezing.

"Take it off. Take it off," she cried the moment Gavin entered the shower, repeating the words as though bugs crawled across her skin.

"I forgive you," he said, a hand wrapped around her waist, breathing against her neck.

"Take it off!" she screamed.

He put a hand on the tile by her face. "This is play, Audrey. I toy with you. It's a game."

"Stop. Stop telling me that. It's all real. *This is real*."

"This is what it's like to truly break. Let me put you back together. I forgive you."

"The line blurs," Audrey said, weeping. "I never know where you end, and *Master* begins."

"I need Peyton. He breaks *me*. You don't think there have been times when I felt like I'm a sick fuck? My own son won't speak to me, Audrey."

"Then just stop all this. Change." Those words were impudent, but she said them anyhow.

"I could no more give this up than I could cease to be a man."

"I'm tired, Gavin..." she said, pausing only to choke back the hyperventilating sounds. "The two of us are coasting on a high we can't sustain. You broke all your own rules with me."

"I fell in love with you."

"You love him too."

"Yes. He knows how to play the game. You're still on the outside looking in. Remember? Two feet. One in, one out. I won't chase you back to domesticity, Audrey. I'm not the hero in a romance novel." He lifted the key from the chain he wore around his neck and unlocked and removed the collar, and then he kissed her on the nape of her neck and placed the necklace in her palm.

"You were always mine," he said and gave her braid three quick tugs.

"Gavin," she cried.

"I'm going to step out and dress, and then I'm leaving the room. Don't come to me tonight unless you plan on staying. Until you're ready to give me both feet."

27

Audrey stood in front of one of the windows, drunk on adren-aline and sick to her stomach from the courage it had taken to show up at Bodhi tonight — free Saturday night, but wasn't every night about freedom? — thinking she could blend into the crowd wearing a black cotton dress. It had drop shoulders and holes, gaping Os in the material at her biceps, her waist, her back.

A scene had been happening for some time now. She could feel the dampness between her legs — not in her panties, because she hadn't worn any.

This was it, wasn't it?

The bottom.

The addict who returned for a fix.

Without her Master to guide her, she felt lost, mostly sick to her stomach, but lost nonetheless.

People crammed in like cattle at the three conjoining windows, fogging the glass, men's dicks stretching their pants, women with hands cupping their wanton triangles.

And tied around Audrey's bicep was a ribbon. A white one.

She could've sworn Gavin kept the AC turned up on purpose. The sadistic son of a bitch wanted people to sweat. He always enjoyed dripping salt onto her face, her breasts. He used to enjoy licking every inch of perspiration from her exhausted, sated body.

Her thighs clenched.

The woman behind the glass sat on her knees, a spreader bar at her shins, keeping her legs wide open and apart. Another bar was fastened behind her biceps while her hands, lying against her supple ass, were clasped. Blood-red pumps and lipstick were the only other things the woman wore. Her tits jutted out, and her nipples were dark, pointing forward. Pretty little peaks made for damaging, taunting, and sucking. Her tangerine-sized breasts were repeatedly being slapped, tweaked, and manipulated by two different people assisting the Dominant.

The luxury on the woman's face made Audrey envious, made her pussy balloon. The pure ecstasy and pain etched on the bitch's face gave Audrey hope she wouldn't leave here tonight without getting what she came for.

What had she come for?

A quick fix? Or something she needed for the rest of her life?

"What do you like?" a man with a throaty voice asked. He stood next to her, but she hadn't really noticed him. He had a tent in his pants like all the others, though. It was hard not to take note of that. *Hard*. Funny, Audrey had made a play on words.

She cleared her throat. "Pardon?"

"What do you like?" he repeated, tipping his head in the direction of the foursome. One of the helpers, another sub, had his cock sliding in and out of her mouth now. Drool spilled from the corners and down her chin. Orders came from the Dom — no one could hear, but his lips moved — who held her head.

And a woman, presumably the third submissive, continued to care for the pretty little breasts beginning to turn a shade of grayish-blue.

"All of it," she whispered.

She caught the stranger sneaking a look at her unbruised back, the dress revealing everything to him but her heart.

"You're pure. White as snow." He flicked his gaze from her skin to the scene. "I can remedy that for you. Tonight, if you'd like. I can find out if another room is open."

"I believe room three is open," Gavin said, and he was behind her now, boxing her in so she couldn't move. With his left hand above and beside her head and his front so close to her back, his presence burned her skin like heat from a thousand suns.

She couldn't move.

Had nowhere to go.

She sagged against the window, and Gavin waited until she righted herself. Fucking bastard wouldn't touch her. Not with his hands. His icy gaze and sardonic words had already cut a deep wound within her soul. She was sure weeks hadn't passed since she'd been near him. Because he felt like home. But he wasn't home. Her body just liked to play tricks with her mind. Pretend she could have both worlds. That she didn't have to choose between this life and the other.

"Would you like me to escort you to room three?" Gavin asked, his lips at her ear.

"Please," the man said, his eyes fixated on the woman being fucked in the face by the helper, slapped and tickled with a flogger by the Dom, and held steady by the third assistant who made sure to fondle and pinch the submissive's greedy little clit.

The Master behind the glass was taking care of what he owned.

Was that why she'd come to Bodhi after weeks of avoiding him?

"Why did you come here tonight?" Gavin flicked the white ribbon on her bicep. The color indicated she was looking for a Dom.

"I missed it," she exhaled, and then he lifted the back of her skirt, causing her to gasp.

"You missed this. You like having your cunt exposed to anyone"—he gave his curt gaze to the man who stood on her right—"who passes by?"

Gavin grabbed her hair, yanking it hard until her forehead faced the ceiling and her eyes watered. "You want *him* to bruise this?"

Him, him, him. Audrey knew who Gavin meant by *him*...

"Do you love him?" Gavin had asked many weeks ago, before she'd safed-out and left him, a night he'd pinned her against the wall with her legs around his waist, his dick in her cunt. She was already breathless from the caning he'd administered and now the pounding. They were in his private room. The dungeon was empty.

It wasn't the first time he'd referred to himself in the third person, and despite the endorphins mounting — his cock buried balls-deep inside the door to her home she always left open for him — she finally understood why he said it.

Like a snake on the prowl, his hand slithered up her chest until he came to a stop at her throat. He clutched it, her collar, her breath, keeping his thumb in the dip.

"Do you love *him*?" He thrust each word into her body.

"Yes," she spluttered. "I do."

He filled her mouth with his fingers, causing her to retch. Drool pooled and spilled as he continued to pummel her as though she were a mere feather pressed into the drywall. Fucking her like an animal on a mission.

"So beautiful," he said, his voice sounding pained. "Being gagged. Being used. Being fucked. It's beautiful."

Eyelids fluttering, kidneys filling with liquid adrenaline, toes bending, she exploded, then became boneless. Only two things kept her upright: her owner and the unforgivable wall.

Gavin continued to fuck her straight through her orgasm, not stopping for her sensitivities, not stopping for her to catch her breath. Sweat rained where they joined, causing them to slip and slide against one another. His jerks became more precise, slowing down, hitting her womb with each entry.

"You think you come here to be made dirty, but you come here to be made clean," he said, and their eyes met. What she saw was too much and so much, and she wanted all of it. "He makes you clean."

"Gavin..." she said, clawing at his backside. Something he'd only recently begun to allow her to do. Dampness covered him there too.

"Clean," he growled. "His cum makes you clean. He makes you clean," he repeated, grunted, and then he filled Audrey up with his purity.

"Do you love him?" he asked with a note of panic in his voice.

He grabbed her face while remaining inside her. His hands cradled her jaw, and Audrey nodded, sobbing without sound. And then he kissed her as hard as he'd fucked her. Bit her. Bruised her. She didn't think he knew how to kiss any other way. And she didn't want him to learn.

Reaching down, he pinched her clit, rubbed it, flicked it until she screamed and bucked. "Call my name when you come. Not *sir*. My name. *Him*."

"Gavin," she cried.

"Yes." He flicked, then pinched her, his semi-hard shaft still filling her up. "Come again."

"Gavin, Gavin..." She squeezed his hips with her thighs. "I love him." And she released for the second time, but not the last, that night.

"Please," Audrey replied to Gavin's question from where they now stood in front of the dungeon window, her ass exposed to anyone who wanted a look. The pliable stranger hadn't moved.

"Get on your knees, Audrey." Gavin dropped the hem of her dress.

"You two have played?" the stranger asked.

"Take out your dick," Gavin said to him in reply.

The man didn't need to be asked twice. Gavin had given an order. An edict. He was the CEO. The Master of this dungeon.

The stranger had his dick out and his hand wrapped around it, his face communicating his allowance of practically anything: a finger in his ass, stripes painted across his skin, humiliation beyond his wildest dreams — maybe he would even bleed. Audrey knew those things to be true because that was how she felt too.

"Don't touch her until I give you permission." Gavin grabbed the man by his base and placed the head of his prick at the edge of Audrey's mouth.

Gavin's own zipper strained. Audrey could smell her Master. His scent brought it all back. The way smells usually did. It wasn't just the smell of his sex. It was him. The cedar, the leather, the shadows. It was him.

Him, him, him, him, him.

God, missing him had morphed into denial, and now the overwhelming onslaught to her senses attempted to usurp it.

She'd grown comfortable in the last several weeks, mistakenly thinking she could live without submission and dominance.

"Why did you come here tonight ... without your fucking collar?"

"Dude, I don't want to—"

"Don't disrespect a man who's literally holding you by the balls. Shut the fuck up." He turned his attention again to Audrey. "Do you want to go to the room with him?" Gavin asked, smearing the man's precum over Audrey's lips. "Don't you dare stick out your fucking tongue. I control this."

Audrey retracted it, moaned, and thought, *Not without you,* as tears began to seep from her lids as she locked onto Gavin's eyes. A lifetime of hurt passed between them. *I'm sorrys* and *I love yous.*

"Find another hole to stick your dick in tonight." Gavin's gaze brooked no room for argument, and the man shoved it in his pants and took a spot at the far end of the window.

"I'll ask you again." Gavin pulled Audrey to stand by the roots of her hair and shoved her face against the glass. "Why did you come here tonight wearing a white ribbon, without my collar, and without anything on under this fucking dress? Do you understand how this works? We check people out, but there are still assholes here waiting to exploit you."

"I know. I'm standing right next to one."

Gavin dropped his chin and feigned a laugh — one Audrey was certain was solely for her benefit. His hand made a trail of sin and fire from her nape to the small of her back.

"How does she look?" He nodded toward the woman behind the glass, but the *she*, like the *him* had been, was in third person. Dual meanings. Nothing simple with Gavin.

"Alive."

"How does she smell?"

"Like the Fourth of July."

"How does she taste?"

"Like one hundred years of women holding signs and begging for rights."

"I should fuck you right here in front of this window." Gavin paused, seeming to wait for her breathing to stabilize. "Did you miss *him*, Audrey? The man who makes you do unspeakable things. Or did you only miss *it*? Not him." Gavin's shell began to crack, his voice giving him away. Tenderness slipped through the fissures. "Do you know what it means to love someone?"

Audrey turned around, hoisted an arm in the air, and made to slap his fucking obstinate face, but Gavin grabbed her wrist. Like clockwork, he snapped the fingers of his other hand, and a man approached.

"Escort her out please," Gavin said to the burly security guy. "She's not welcome here anymore. Make a note. Inform the staff."

"Yes, sir."

Gavin had already walked away.

However, Audrey knew, despite his posture — upright and forward, tight and disciplined — he was an outstanding piece of clay waiting to be reshaped or made new.

And wasn't that what she was too?

Why had she come to Bodhi tonight?

Driven by unspeakable desires? Yes. But the love in her heart — she knew what it was to love someone — tore a hole in her chest. Loving Gavin meant living without him ... but it didn't mean she'd have to live without Bodhi — because she'd stumbled upon enlightenment, and it wasn't confined to walls or thrones or crosses.

She just didn't know what to do with her newfound knowledge.

Right now, she couldn't choose him or the dungeon — she had to focus on what she'd begun to unearth:

Herself.

But even so, Gavin would always own Audrey — every fucking last bit of her heart and soul and mind and body. Her Master had ruined her for any other.

Audrey decided she believed in purgatory.

28

Audrey had found out from Kate.

Even though they hadn't spoken all summer — it had been a few months since Gavin banned her from Bodhi. And she'd been ignoring Kate's text messages ... or trying to. The last set, the ones she reread in the dark of night, had come in a group of six. Back to back, but separate, and all shot off in a matter of minutes...

Kate: It's on your terms. I won't push you.

I miss your friendship. Your smile.

I'm not supposed to tell you, but he's miserable.

Darcy is begging him to sell again, but he doesn't know how to cut the cord.

Come back to us, Audrey.

I love you.

The newest message was from this morning, though, and it couldn't be ignored.

Kate: Michael is in ICU. Bayfront. Room 413. Gavin is on his way now. Just found out.

Audrey left work early. After stepping out of the elevator onto the fourth floor of the hospital, she picked up the beige phone attached to the wall, told the nurse who she was visiting, and then she hung up and gained access to the intensive care unit.

Paintings of Christ lined the walls. Quoted scripture mixed with hospital lingo. Some patient doors were open, some closed. Staff moved about.

And then she saw him.

Standing in front of the room housing his injured son — his nose pressed to the glass, his shoulders slumped, his ramrod spine slouching — was the man she hadn't stopped loving or wanting or needing.

Audrey stepped behind the nurses' station and watched, not ready to interrupt his meditation.

"His wife just stepped out a moment, sir," Audrey heard a nurse say to Gavin. "You're here to see Michael?"

"Wife?" Gavin tripped over the word. It had sputtered from his lips in the form of a question. He hadn't taken his hand from his pocket. He seemed to be playing with something — keys or change. "I'm, uh..." He looked from the nurse to Michael.

"Please, sir, why don't you step out into the waiting area, and I'll let Mrs. Sellers know that you're here."

Mrs. Sellers, Audrey thought as she scrambled to make her way to the double doors before he did. Playing and picking at her lips, she began to pace in the hallway. Gavin hadn't known his son had a wife. That revelation and Kate's latest text message played on a loop in her mind...

Kate: Gavin saw it on the news, Audrey. The fucking news.

And then the automatic doors opened.

Audrey stopped fidgeting, composed herself, and stood stock still as the man on the other side of the threshold observed her waiting for him. Ready for him. Anything for him.

Gavin took four large steps and embraced her, almost

knocking her off her feet, burying his head so far into her neck as he began to shake with the sobs he'd held back moments before. She stroked the back of his neck, pinched his skin there, rubbed his earlobe. He wet her shirt and skin with his tears.

The double doors opened, startling them, and they separated. A petite woman passed, entering the ICU, wearing up-to-the-knee leather cowboy boots. Audrey only caught the brown boots and the swish of her skirt before the doors closed again.

"The waiting room," Audrey tipped her head toward it, and Gavin followed.

It was empty. Only chairs and tables and a single television. A needless distraction of talking heads from the imminent uncertainty of the hospital rooms. Gavin shoved a hand into his pocket again. He was definitely fondling something. She could see an outline of what he touched.

"Peyton?" he asked.

"Kate."

He nodded.

"I'm so—" she began and started to step forward, but he put up a hand and stopped her movement and speech.

"Thank you for coming."

"Do you know anything?" Audrey asked even though she knew he didn't.

Moments ago, near the nurses' station, seemed to have been the only time Gavin had been unaware of her presence in a room.

"No." One hand remained in his pocket, and the other scratched at the back of his neck.

They were silent a moment.

"Go home, Audrey," he said in the voice she knew well. Her Master. The commander. The purveyor of her land. The broken man still managed to compose himself.

"This is real fucking life," he said, his shaky voice putting a chink in his armor. "This is what you want?"

They exchanged a look only two people who knew each other's ins and outs could share: his poignant and devastated and hers open and open and open.

"Every moment with you"—she swallowed—"has been real, Gavin."

"Go home, baby girl." He tugged at her loose braid hanging over her right shoulder.

"No."

"I don't want you here."

"Bullshit." She held her head high, met his eyes with an assurance. "I'm not wearing your co—necklace. I'm not taking orders."

"Exactly," he said, his eyes snapping back to hers and then landing on her bare neck. "I said not until you were ready *with both feet.*"

"I'm not leaving until you speak with Michael's wife." Audrey folded her arms across her chest.

Gavin's eyes bulged with vulnerability — splintered red and glossy, a sea of blue grief. "You ask without knowing the question. You seek without knowing what you search for."

"Ask and it shall be given. Seek and you shall find."

He cracked a smile at her choice of reply.

Audrey imagined reaching out and touching his cheek, caressing his skin, kissing his lips and telling him, *Be brave, Gavin, I love you.*

But that moment had come and gone.

———

"'Don't be afraid,' the prophet answered. 'Those who are with us are more than those who are with them.' And Elisha prayed, 'Open his eyes, LORD, so that he may see.'"

After speaking the verses, Gavin dropped his head, pinching a finger and thumb into the corners of his eyes. Audrey placed a hand on the small of his back, and he continued.

"'Then the LORD opened the servant's eyes, and he looked and saw the hills full of horses and chariots of fire all around Elisha.'"

Gavin stopped reciting the scripture as though it were a prayer — the one Audrey had never heard. He seemed to be waiting for a miracle to occur.

The woman in the room with Michael turned from the window she'd been staring out of, giving them a frontal view of a belly full of child.

Gavin met the woman's gaze, his eyes still swollen and red, also tired and restitute. The pregnant woman's eyes were aware, as if she'd known this moment was coming, had anticipated it, and now accepted it.

The wife with child, looking all of about twenty-two or -three, walked toward the door, past the noise of the machines, past her unconscious husband — the son of a man she'd never met — her brown hair swaying in the ponytail, her cowboy boots tapping the tile. "Gavin," she whispered hoarsely the moment she stepped into the hall.

He nodded and said, "I'm sorry," then cleared his throat. "I don't know—"

"I'm Sarah." She extended her hand, and he shook it. Then he resumed stroking the thing in his pocket. "The doctors say it's uncertain at this point. He's in an induced coma."

Gavin covered his mouth. His hand trembled in front of his face. His eyes watered. "Can I? May I go in?"

Sarah peered into the room. "The staff doesn't want him

under stress. He may be aware of everything that's said or happens."

Gavin inhaled. "I understand. I'm, uh ... this is Audrey."

"Hello." Audrey smiled with a Princess Diana delicacy and nodded. "Can I get you anything to eat? Or anything?"

"I've been forcing myself to eat..." Sarah thumbed her belly while Audrey swallowed guilt and sorrow. "My mother's coming soon." She glanced at the clock on the screen of her phone. "Michael's mother is on her way too."

"Can you give my son this?" Gavin retrieved what looked like a homemade angel from his pocket and handed it to his daughter-in-law. He cried without shame, making no sounds as tears slid down his face. "And can you message me, please?"

Sarah took a deep breath. "Of course, Mr. Sellers." She kindly took the origami angel from him, then she opened the screen on her phone.

"It's Gavin. Please."

After typing in his name — Audrey peeked — as Grandpa Gavin, she handed him the phone. His hands were still possessed with the trembling as he punched in the digits.

"He made that," Gavin said as he returned the device, his eyes on the silver angel. "We made it together. I think he was nine or ten." He inhaled, palming his scruff. "It shouldn't stress him."

"No..." Her voice held a note of wistfulness. "It will make him happy. I'll make sure, Mr. ... Gavin"—Sarah smiled and wiped away tears—"it's in the palm of his hand. I'll tell him what it is."

Gavin nodded and said thank you with such reverence and fortitude; his polite words seemed to contain all his hope and belief that his prayers would indeed be answered.

And for the first time in a long time — or maybe ever — Audrey wished to put faith in the unknown.

29

"Why did you pick me up early?"

"I wanted to see you, Rick."

Audrey's eyes were red-rimmed behind her sunglasses as she pulled out of the Catholic school parking lot. God would understand. God would forgive her.

I forgive you. She heard Gavin's words from not that many months ago and felt his lips against her skin in the shower — the day she'd begged him to remove the collar, the day he'd told her not to come back without both feet — and she shivered. Bit her tongue so she wouldn't cry.

"Stephanie said they're going to the fair this weekend. I wanna go. Bryson won't hang out with me there. Can we go with Stephanie?"

Audrey snuck a hand beneath the shades and wiped a film of tears away.

"Mommy, why are you crying?"

Nothing slipped past Ricki. Well, nothing slipped by either of her perceptive boys, but Rick wasn't afraid to ask. Bryson had stopped making inquiry by age ten. Dell had given up as well ...

and at some point in their marriage, ignorance had become bliss. Maybe that was when the curtain really fell.

Empathy wasn't something Audrey wanted to manufacture. And the organic "How are you today, babe? Why are you upset? What can I do to make it better?" had disappeared. Dell had wanted his own validation too. And who could've blamed him? The kids had sucked every ounce of ready-made empathy Audrey had left to dole out.

"My friend," she began, swallowing the gunk collecting in her nasal cavity, "his son is in the hospital."

Rick was silent. Audrey chanced a glance at him in the rearview.

"Is he okay?" he finally asked.

Audrey squeezed the wheel like it was one of those balls people squished at their office desks. The ones meant to relieve stress. The wheel had no give, though ... like her mind.

"Umm..." Her voice trembled. "We don't know, buddy. I picked you up early because"—*I love you and needed to see you and I need a comfort right now I have no right to ask you for because you're a little boy but you're so sweet and precious and I need to hear your voice and know YOU ARE alive with my own two eyes*—"I want to make something with you."

After buying some supplies at the craft store, Audrey and Rick sat at the dining table looking at images on his tablet. Pictures of angels and fire. Heavens full of armies.

"Do you know this story, buddy?"

"Yeah." He was cutting up pieces of construction paper into strange shapes.

Audrey hadn't at first remembered it. Hearing Gavin recite the verses today had put her in a state of limbo. These were the times she needed God. Wanted His protection. Did that make her a bad human creation? Did she only want Him when things were tough?

"What do you think it means?" Audrey asked Rick as though he were a pastor or an oracle who had all the answers. And she did have a vague idea, but she wanted to gauge his reaction.

He shrugged and continued cutting. "We haven't been to the fair in a long time, Mom. Stephanie wants—"

"Rick, please." She squeezed his wrist. "We'll go to the fair—"

"Yes!"

"Please focus on this."

"Mom, I do school stuff all day."

"I know, but I picked you up early. I need your help."

"Why?"

"Because you know things. What does the story about Elisha mean to you?" They'd already read the verses out loud before they found pictures online.

He sighed and repeated what he must've learned by rote. "We have a whole lot more help when we're being hurt than we realize."

Audrey's eyes widened, turning into sunbeams.

"Those angels prove it." Rick had been relaying his wisdom while he concentrated on whatever artistic expression he was inventing with the paper, markers, and glue. But his tone and words belied his preoccupation.

"Do you believe in them? Angels?"

"Sure. Just cause ya can't see them doesn't mean they ain't there." He stopped coloring. "Mom?"

Audrey tried to hood her eyes, wishing she'd worn her sunglasses inside the house. She tried to never let the kids see her cry. Only the mattress saw that ... and the pillow.

"Mommy. It will be okay." Rick stood and gave her a hug.

"It will," she said, full of certainty, tear ducts now dry — remembering the faith on Gavin's weary face earlier in the ICU gave her strength. "I have an idea. You take this shiny paper and cut out circles, like this."

30

The gumption it took for Audrey to drive to Tampa a few days later was an asset she subconsciously knew she possessed.

The whys and hows.

Audrey just did things.

Moved forward.

Went along.

She distracted herself with enough of the ordinary but necessary in life, that it took quite a bit to knock her off the log or boat or wagon. Pick a metaphor.

Audrey had survived her mother's cancer.

Audrey had survived her *Splendor in the Grass* depression.

Audrey had survived divorce.

Life was a series of paddles. *What do you call those boats on the Mississippi? The one at the Magic Kingdom that takes you around Tom Sawyer's Island?*

A paddle steamer.

A riverboat.

Powered by a steam engine that drives paddlewheels to propel the craft through the water.

Yeah. Those.

Life was those paddles. Circling and recycling and powering forward.

The same constant motion.

But it moves you.

Changes your direction if it wants to. But it keeps on going.

Audrey was a paddle.

Hmm. A paddle...

Utilizing his favorite paddle, Gavin had painted Audrey's butt cheeks bright red one day several months ago, leaving her skin broken and stinging from the lashes — a strike for each day he'd been without her that month.

Gavin had decided she deserved the punishment, they both did, and doling out marks for her absence had become a regular scene they looked forward to. It reminded her of the chasm, the bridge they still needed to build ... or the one they'd constructed and would burn down.

Which would it be? Which had it been?

Eyes stern and bright, his dick out but his pants still on, Gavin sat in the chair in his room and snapped his fingers. He seemed to watch with keen interest as Audrey — naked and aware — crawled to him, resuming her ready position inches from his feet. Obeying made her pulse and throb.

"Did you know certain civilizations worshipped a man's cock?" he asked as he lifted it at the base. "Lingam and Yoni. Drukpa Kunley. The Egyptian god Min. You're to study this."

"Yes, sir."

"Make me hard."

With his hand holding his semi-hard dick up, Audrey took over and began to pump him until he grew stiffer and longer, until he turned to motherfucking steel. Regarding her curiously, peering at her as if she were actually beneath him — not just physically — his sharp-as-a-blade interest seemed to be replaced with the observation of a man learning the codes to an arsenal of deadly weapons.

Ready to strike.

Ready to impose.

"You will worship my cock." He pointed to the floor using his head and then swiveled a hand, indicating she pay him obeisance.

"Worship my cock, Audrey. Bow."

She lowered her head, arched her back, and prostrated herself. Closing her eyes, she breathed in the smell of the cold concrete floor and the scent of his arousal while imagining looks she'd seen swimming through the Copenhagen stream of his blue eyes. Gazes — a man opening his soul ... a man on the verge of transcendence — she'd memorized.

Gavin Sellers' domination spun on a pinwheel founded upon desire. And each tip pointed at her.

"Up," he said with a pinch of coldness she admired and a strangling authority she craved like catnip. "Suck me."

As she welcomed him to the back of her throat, she licked and sucked and moaned, focusing on breathing and pleasing while moving her tongue then repeating ... until her jaw ticked and ached and her eyes watered.

"Is that the best you can do?" He cupped her chin. "Really?" Sarcasm colored his voice, and she became unsure of the game. It always felt so real. Too real. And wasn't that why she played? "I allow you the privilege of sucking me without fucking your little face"—he yanked her hair—"and this is the *best* you can do?"

He held onto the strands, pulling on them until she yelped around his cock, causing her to consciously remind herself not to clamp her teeth around him.

"Suck. Me."

Appearing utterly disinterested — though she knew he was

anything but because his voice was clipped and harsh, volatile and vulnerable — he dropped her hair, leaned back, and gripped the chair with a firmness she could see in his arms. His restraint was apparent in each muscle of his body, each bulging vein. She could read the fierce control he gave up in writing across his exposed skin, tight and boiling just under the surface.

"I could order ten people in here," he groaned. "Women or men who would give anything to suck me off. Do you understand? *No one* sucks me unless I grant them the privilege. And even then, *no one* has control," he hissed as she began in earnest again.

"Worship this cock," he said without thrusting his hips. "Some people say a blowjob is for the receiver and cock worship for the giver. I say it's both, Audrey. This is for us. I gift you other cocks. I share you, but *you will worship mine* because it's yours. You honor me. This. Us."

His words came out in broken syllables now. And it all drove her insane with need. It was enough to make her forget the ache in her womb, the tick in her jaw, and the sear on her ass cheeks.

But she didn't want to forget.

The pain was a catalyst. Necessary to drive the engine. Lips fierce around the head of her Master, Audrey moaned in pleasure as she consumed him, wanting only to worship and serve and swallow his dick until there was nothing left of her doubts and fears and conclusions.

Sucking cock had become a spiritual exercise for Audrey. A ritual. Gavin had learned this; maybe he had taught her, encouraged her to explore it. His knowing what she needed without her having to always verbalize it was the reason he'd afforded her so many men to suck and lick, the reason he cherished watching the cum of play partners hit her body, why he often spread and massaged it into her skin like a luxurious cream.

Cum was a sacrament.

Go ahead. Deny it. Defy it. Say that it's wrong.

Audrey couldn't do that anymore. And with that realization and acceptance came enlightenment. A spiritual awakening. The act itself — sucking, licking, filling mouth to the brim with a man's most vulnerable piece of skin, muscle, and organ — had become sacred to her.

Anytime she found herself lying with Gavin, resting at his feet, in or out of scene, she wanted to and often did put her mouth on him. It pacified her conscience, relieved stress. His dick in her mouth wasn't only about the act of sex or anticipated stimulation or release.

And it was for both of them.

Without warning, Gavin yanked her head off his prick.

"Stick out your tongue," he said, one hand holding her braid in his grip, the other pumping his slick, revered cock while chanting, "Mine. Mine. Mine." He repeated the four-letter opus as he ejaculated onto her hair and cheeks, lips and tongue.

"Fuck!" he yelled — no, growled — and then he kissed the braids, marking the strands as his, kissing her as though he were anointing her, praising her as though he were worshiping *her*, and then he lifted her into his arms and cradled her as he reclined.

Laying across his bare chest, her feet dangling over the chair's arm, his sweet, sticky seed covering her hair and face, her lips bee-stung, she barely noticed him slipping one finger over her clit and two others into her wet hole.

"Shhh," he said, quieting her shakes, fingering her slowly, touching the sensitive spot on the inside of her wall. "The best. My best." His digits slid in and then out, stroking her clit to hole. "My baby girl." Each word was a whisper and a promise.

Face planted at his neck for safekeeping, she began to cry as she opened her legs wider — without shame, asking for more of what he offered.

"That's right, baby girl," he said to soothe her. "My cock belongs to you. Only you own it. Yes?"

She nodded, making incoherent sounds. "Did you mean...?"

"Shhh," he repeated against her cheeks as she shook in his arms, as she cried without any reservation. "No. I open old wounds. Humiliate you because I can. You bleed for me, and sometimes the hurt is where no one else can see it. Only God. And me." He kissed her collar and the skin underneath. "I love you, baby girl."

Her seismic release happened at *that* moment with *those* words, and it spread to every nerve in her body. The orgasm couldn't be confined to her pussy. Like dominos on fire, each block dropped, enflaming and engorging everything as her contractions milked his fingers.

This was what she needed.

Who she needed.

All she needed.

People who disagreed, didn't know. Couldn't understand. If she could be lucky enough to live to a ripe old age without having experienced this — *this, this, this* — ascension to a universe existing beyond every known world man manufactures and creates, then living would've been for naught.

This was the purpose all great teachers over the centuries spoke of.

Satisfying the desire of every living thing until there was no more want.

The meaning of life.

She'd found her Bodhi.

And now she'd arrived at the dungeon. It was time to put away the memories. She stood at the service entrance and rang the bell.

"God, kid," Darcy said after opening the door — Darcy's feet inside and Audrey's out. "Look at you. Your hair looks a little shorter. Cute."

"And yours is gray, Darc."

"You like it?" She turned her head side to side. "Gray is the new purple."

It never mattered what color Darcy chose for her hair — gray, blue, purple, orange — they all reminded Audrey of Jem from *The Holograms*.

"It's chic." Audrey smiled, swinging the gift bag she held in her hand.

The women stared at one another. Darcy's gaze saying, *I'm not supposed to let you in. Does he know you're here?* Her expression also seemed to betray a secret, something else regarding Gavin...

Perhaps the selling of the club Kate had mentioned? Fuck, Audrey needed to talk to Kate. She'd been a piece of shit, avoiding her calls and texts for most of the summer.

"How's Michael?" Audrey cleared her throat. It had only been a few days since the accident — a fucking hit-and-run.

"He's awake," a voice said from behind, causing Audrey to nearly burst into tears at the sound of its bass.

Gavin stood behind Darcy, a small, white towel over his shoulder, secrets in his eyes, and a placid mask in place he no doubt wore for her benefit.

Audrey wanted to kneel, spread her knees, and present her wrists and palms for her Master. The yearning was immediate. She longed for a generous pet from his hand. A stroke of his fingers across her cheek, shoulder, neck. "Good girl" to fall from his lips. His eyes to inspect every inch of her body. To claim her as his. She needed his approval and the trust and protection that came with it.

The need was like a spark waiting to detonate into fireworks.

"I'm getting ready to go there now. I'm leaving." He spoke so matter-of-factly. So full of utter bullshit. But they had made an agreement. *Don't come to me unless it's with both feet.* And he could surely tell she wasn't standing before him now with two feet. Nor had she been when she'd disgracefully entered the club the night he'd forbidden her to return.

Gavin could read Audrey like a charm. Always could.

One foot in the "real" world and another in his fucking iron-clad heart.

"I came to give you something," Audrey said, and then Darcy excused herself after giving Audrey a friendly peck on the cheek.

Gavin eyed the spot on the ground where Audrey stood: both feet still outside in the heat. He didn't ask her to come inside. Nor did he reply.

"Is he out of ICU?"

"No. He's making progress, though. He just started eating solids."

"You've spoken?"

"Audrey, what do you need?"

To be taken over his knee. To eat floor or mattress, to have her body painted with bruises and welts, to shake with freedom, to release fears, to feel her face stream with tears. To lie at his feet.

He orchestrated her pain. He understood the submission. And then no one else could have power over the demons trying to surface.

"I said I brought you something. Rick made it. We both did. And there's something else in here for the baby."

He took the gift bag from her hands without touching her skin.

She glanced away and swallowed, then looked back at him — in the fucking eyes — and told him how much she did indeed love him without words.

She knew what it was to love someone. Gavin had said that merely to test her, to press her. And she'd failed.

Was this how Dell had felt when she'd hurt him?

The heartache over leaving Gavin hadn't stopped. Hadn't gone away.

It wasn't fantasy. Or make believe.

The collar, their non-arranged arrangement, was every bit as real as her *I do* had been with her husband. It didn't matter that Gavin and Audrey hadn't properly courted or held hands.

Standing this close to her owner didn't just ignite every nerve in her body — it made her soul come alive too. Made her know without a fucking doubt she was a strong person. Had goals. Had reasons. Had things worth saying and doing and expressing. And leaving him today ... when she had to walk away again...

Audrey looked at the ground ... the threshold she refused to cross. Then her eyes combed his entire body from his toes to his face. Once she reached the starry-night sky of his Copenhagen eyes, she turned, shifting on her axis, ready to depart.

"Audrey," he said, his voice laced with pain, an ache ... love.

"I'm here," she choked out but kept going forward like the paddles on the riverboat.

31

Audrey found herself alone inside her tiny walk-in closet. A few weeks had passed since the horrific accident. And in that time, Audrey had worked things out with Kate.

Kate kept her informed of Michael's progress. He was home. And he *was* seeing his dad, talking to him — which made Audrey's heart swell ten times its size. He had a long way to go on his road to recovery, though, but Kate said his prognosis was quite good. Soon, Michael and Sarah's baby would be born too. Gavin would be a grandfather.

Enough time passes ... and life changes.

Faith moves mountains.

Gavin had meant what he'd said about the two feet and the real life. After Audrey had given him the handmade craft and baby gift, after she'd walked away from Bodhi for the third time, he'd never attempted contact, and neither had she.

At first, Audrey thought she was fine. Only a thin film of dust had settled over her soul. Nothing permanent. Nothing she couldn't remove with a fancy feather duster named optimistic hope and faith in the unknown future. But she had to wear a mask for her sons.

However, as time wore on ... the dust didn't just settle; it caked, fell in between cracks and crevices she hadn't known existed, fucking up the wires inside her already fucked-up brain. And she realized the things in her life she'd thought were only part of the past hadn't ever really gone away.

The divorce she'd not truly mourned.

The mother she continued to mourn every day — each November a reason to wish for the pain in her chest to deflate. The previous month's (October) push of pink-ribbon-wearing cancer survivors a reminder of the hurt that never truly left.

Her children who didn't have a father under the same roof and deserved one.

Her failed attempts at anything resembling normal.

Gavin...

Audrey knew why she'd come into the closet. But it took her several minutes of catching her breath before she could pull the weekender off the shelf. The bag she'd stowed away behind a plastic container full of wrapping paper, tissues, and bows several months ago.

Knowing what she would find...

She could feel the item's energy pass through the thick material.

She opened the zipper and removed the wrinkly clothes. What she'd tried to leave behind had been with her all along...

Dropping to a lotus position in the center of her closet, she clutched the silver collar in her hands and cried tears she'd forbidden. And she cried for two days straight. Days in which she...

Took off work. Sent the boys to her father's. Couldn't eat. Couldn't function. An exhaustion the worst she'd known since pregnancy.

And to top it off, fantasizing about Gavin had increased.

The commands. The boundary pushing. The sharing. The

smell of his skin. The feel of him. His warm chest. His fucking arms — brute and wide and soft.

If only he would hold her in *this* side of the world. If only he would give up heaven to join her on earth.

He had to be missing her.

He had to have moved on.

He had Peyton.

He had an endless supply of sexual freaks willing to beg so they might serve him, be beaten by him ... maybe even be collared by him.

But did he have a *woman* to love him?

Did he see in others' eyes what she saw in his?

Would she ever see that again in this lifetime?

Could she find it this side of reality?

Could she phone him?

His words — *don't come back to me until you're ready to give me both feet* — played over and over in her mind. What did they really mean?

It meant giving herself to him without borders. Presenting herself whole in mind and spirit — because he didn't want only her body. It meant not denying her children or choosing between them and him. When she offered him her love and devotion, they weren't supposed to come with stipulations. It meant accepting the two of them as they were ... not how she wished for them to be.

It meant she had to stop expecting him to enter her world.

As she sat in the closet clutching her submission to one man, she found herself beginning to think of another...

Both men *she'd let go.*

Dell's aura surrounded her in the tiny closet they used to share. The smell of his skin after he shaved. The way his dark hair felt between her fingers. The taste of his tongue after he smoked, then brushed his teeth. And of course, the damn crinkles around his eyes.

In these moments, she didn't dwell on what their marriage had become. In these moments, she wondered if she'd ever truly allowed herself to feel any of this since they'd separated. Because thinking about the past made her miss the things she could depend on. The things she romanticized made her long for a time only existing in her memory. But what was broken couldn't be put back together with wishful thinking.

Monumental things they'd shared together seemed so long ago...

"Come on, ABS, push."

"Keep her legs steady," the maternity ward nurse said to Dell.

Audrey had managed to remember that exchange when most words said the night Bryson had been born ended up as part of a haze of sweat rolling off her forehead, part of a boulder the size of Jupiter about to break free and roll out from between her legs.

Out of her mind and unable to do anything but focus on the pain — it had been too late for an epidural — Audrey had felt each and every sensation.

The grinding against her lower backside. The stinging. The heat. The ascent of a particularly strong contraction rising, then peaking, and the shaking that followed.

She didn't want to forget any of it.

Wore it like a badge of honor.

A privilege.

She must've squeezed Dell's hands hard enough to have hurt them, probably slung curses at him, but he never complained. His eyes, blue and filling with a soon-to-be-a-father goo, framed by his trademark crinkles, warmed her head to toe. His smile did too. He kept her from falling over the edge of panic.

And before she knew it, she'd crowned, pushing a squirmy

little body through a passage that had stretched to an ungodly size. And then, the uniformed-staff laid a perfect tiny baby across her fluctuating chest.

Dell stared at Bryson.

Audrey had never seen anything like it ... a father's reverence. She saw it again when Rick was born. And again, in the ICU, brimming over in Gavin's heartbroken paternal gaze. Unconditional love from men who would've desecrated anything standing between them and their sons.

Audrey had destroyed her family's bond — *what God has yoked together let no man put asunder* — and given up on Dell ... fell out love and like and lust.

How was she any different from Gavin's son?

The chain in her hand felt like lead as she brought the collar to her cheek and rubbed it across her skin.

After a few more moments spent with the symbol she'd grown accustomed to, wanted and needed, she went into her bedroom and placed the necklace in her jewelry box, then stared at the wall. Not at the pictures or knickknacks, only the wall.

Thoughts swam though her mind, morphing into a whirlpool of emotions.

Dad had the children, took them to school and practice, while she ran away from responsibility.

Audrey had the bed and her thoughts and her tears and her failures.

Her father had been the one who'd finally broached the subject of her sadness when she'd dropped off the boys this past Sunday afternoon. Because depression never seemed like depression when one was in the thick of it. Or it did, but she didn't call it depression. Didn't label it or name it because then she would have to do something about it.

But the boys knew. Rick had mentioned it first actually. Audrey hadn't done as good a job hiding her initial layer of dust as she'd thought.

"What do you wish for, Rick?" she had asked him a few nights ago while tucking the blankets toward his chin. She'd just finished reading him one of his favorite books: The Boy Who Fooled the Giant.

He yawned. "If I tell you, it won't come true."

"It's not a birthday cake, buddy." Nudging him, she kissed his cheek and tugged on the covers. *"The boy in the story made his own wishes come true."*

"I wish..." He hesitated a moment, and Audrey couldn't imagine why. *"I wish for you to be happy again."* He closed his eyes.

"Oh, baby," she said and sighed, unable to fight the sandpaper scratching her throat as she kissed his cheek again. *"Look at me, Rick."* She wiped tears from the corners of her eyes. *"I love you."*

"I love you, too."

"Mommy is happy every time I see you."

And then on Sunday ... her father had pulled her into his bedroom, and closed the door...

"I haven't seen you like this since before..." He nodded toward the living room where the boys were. *"Since high school, Bean."*

"I'm fine. It's just a funk."

Her father tapped the spot next to him on the bed, and she followed. *"Rick says you're crying all the time."*

"Kids make stuff up, Dad. I cry ... a little. He exaggerates."

"We never see your friend Kate anymore. Were you and her? She and you?"

Raising a trembling hand to her lips, Audrey swallowed and tried to stop her eyes from watering. She shook her head and just let the drops of salt fall. She didn't bother to wipe them.

"It is about a relationship, though?"

"It's so complicated, Dad," she said, sucking in a deluge of air through her nose.

He patted her knee, then wiped her cheeks. "I don't need details,

Butterbean. I need you to do something about this. It's been long enough. Go see someone. Get some medication."

When he'd finished speaking, she'd dried her eyes and sniffled, trying to suck all the sadness away the way she tried to do so now in the middle of her bedroom, trying to hide truth. But she could never keep it from her father.

Dad had never been a typical man.

When Mom died, he didn't start chasing women. Her father was too busy keeping the business of *living* up and running.

The disease had changed him, of course. The way it had changed Audrey, her mom's brother and sister, and grandmommy. Audrey had only just come out of the teenage-onset depression a few years before her mom's diagnosis. Stopped sleeping with her clothes on until two o'clock in the afternoon. Stopped eating ham on rye — smeared in Miracle Whip, not mayonnaise — with the crusts cut off because it was the only fucking food she could swallow and chew. Half a sandwich because a whole two pieces of bread proved to be too daunting, made her stomach swirl just looking at it.

She'd been fifteen. Had to stop going to school. Took up correspondence. Earned her GED. Took time off between that and college. Did the whole dental assistant thing later.

No one had medicated her at fifteen and sixteen.

No one had called it depression. No one had a name for the thing that followed her around and suffocated her, despised her.

She'd learned to pretend. How to keep her emotions between the lines.

Each time she swallowed food, it was a victory. Each time she woke up without her stomach in knots and filled with an ocean of butterflies, it was a miracle. Friends distracted her.

And she'd sworn that when her mom had been diagnosed with stage four ovarian cancer, she wasn't going to eat ham sandwiches ever again. By then, she'd had Bryson too. A little child depended on her. Dell still needed her love and affection. Still held her hand. Actually, Dell held her hand through the entire ordeal.

And that was a horrible word for watching her mother *not* survive cancer. *Ordeal.*

Weathering a storm can make one stronger, or it can shake an already wonky foundation off its axis.

Dell and Audrey were the latter.

His hand couldn't hold their marriage together.

Dad helped put Audrey back together.

Both times.

By the time she'd turned seventeen, she could no longer hide the moods. She'd lost weight. Withdrawn so much she barely spoke to anyone. Her father sent her to an outpatient program. Used some of his hard-earned savings.

And then, years later, after Mom passed, he moved to Spring Hill to be closer to Audrey and the boys. He started looking after them, taking them places: spring training and Marvel movies — being the grandparent she knew he wished his wife could've seen.

Dad didn't chase rainbows, and he didn't ask Audrey why she'd started to do so when Kate came into the picture. Never asked who they spent time with on the weekends. Never complained about the parenting skills Audrey often felt she lacked. Never scolded her for divorcing Dell.

Both father and daughter needed the isolation and the comfort. Both needed to know the other was merely there — without pressure or overt commitment. They coexisted. Made it through each day. They did whatever they could to be everything for the boys.

Maybe I am an okay mother.

Okay ... more than okay.

She had to take credit somewhere for something.

She found it was often the mothers who never thought they did enough, chastising themselves for never measuring up, who were usually doing far too much.

Bryson and Rick handed out smiles all summer by the dozen — even as Audrey felt herself slipping closer and closer to another version of sixteen-year-old, fucked-up, lost-and-lonely, ham-and-cheese-sandwich, Miracle-Whip Audrey.

Two in the afternoon on a Tuesday.

Having called in sick from work again.

Distracted.

Sinking.

Audrey.

But this was different.

Still depression but different.

Like floating above the water in the middle of a large pond instead of drowning in the insurmountable ocean.

Her father had been right — as usual. She would have to ask the PCP for medication, but first she would find somewhere she could lie on a couch, a person with a license she could talk to.

32

"What do you want?"

"To be a good mother. To be happy."

"Aren't you both those things?"

"Sometimes."

"No one is all things ... all the time."

A pause filled the room. Not an awkward one, the contemplative kind. Memories of what it meant to be happy flitted through Audrey's mind.

"When did this start, Audrey? What was the catalyst?"

"I don't even know anymore. I thought..." She paused. "I thought it was when I met Gavin." Everything was muddled. What she wanted to say she couldn't seem to voice. It was all there ... somewhere in the recesses of her brain.

"Tell me about Gavin."

The therapist had the basic facts, and now she wanted the emotions — the driving force. She wanted Audrey to cut open her own chest and rip out her heart.

"But now ... I don't even know. I think it started"—Audrey paused again, her wheels visibly turning—"way before. Gavin is ... was ... my Master."

"You were his slave?"

"He didn't usually ... there are varying degrees of... I..."

"Take your time. You know I'm familiar with the dynamics, but I want to hear yours."

"I don't want to talk about Gavin."

"How long ago did things end with Gavin?"

"Things will never end with Gavin. He owns me," Audrey said, and then stopped abruptly. After standing up, she shifted and paced.

"Sit down, Audrey."

"Please," she said with a strain.

"Please what?"

"I don't know. Make this noise in my head stop. This catch in my throat."

"I don't prescribe medication."

"I don't want medication!" Audrey screamed the words and then balled up the tissue in her fist and resumed sitting. She knew she needed the fucking medication ... only she was putting it off.

Once her breathing regulated, she said, "I was never like this with my husband." Crazy in love. Unable to imagine never seeing him again. Wishing to share every secret: the good and bad.

"Dell," the therapist said, speaking his name like he was a clinical observation and not the father of her children.

"Yes. *Dell*. I loved him, but it wasn't like this. This ... God ... this fucking pain. It hurts everywhere. Everything hurts." She clutched her throat. "This," she said, clawing at her neck, "it aches. Like it's swollen. All the time. Like I'm sick, but I'm not. It's throbbing pain. I can't eat. My stomach—"

"Audrey..."

"Please?" Audrey said, although she didn't even know what she begged for. No one had an answer. Being with Gavin hadn't been one. Their relationship had been a gag order, a drain stopper for this bullshit vomiting out of her now at the speed of light.

Was it wrong that Audrey needed order and discipline? Welts and lashes and commands? If only the therapist would tell her what to do. But it wouldn't matter. Wasn't that right? Dell could've demanded Audrey do things. He could've pushed her. And she might've only laughed at his attempt at dominance.

The therapist handed her another tissue. "He represents something for you."

"What?" Audrey replied, not wishing to believe her. She wanted her ears tickled.

"Gavin's a figure to you. He makes other pain, things you've stored away for a rainy day and refused to deal with since you were"—she looked at her notes—"fifteen ... seem okay to keep reticent."

"I had treatment."

"You learned to cope with pain? Or you used, or continue to use, distraction? Medication? You're highly functional."

"Fuck this," Audrey said and stood.

"Is this how you cope? You avoid conversation about things that hurt? Sit down, please. I want to talk to you."

Audrey scoffed. "I don't know you. Why should I talk to you?"

"Was this your choice? Coming here?"

"My father suggested it." *Everything is my choice.* "I found you. I chose you. I didn't refute or argue with his suggestion."

"But you disagreed? Did you want to come to therapy? Do you want to talk openly about your feelings?"

Audrey dropped onto the sofa, pressed her palms into the cushion, and began to rock. Not crazy rocking, but subtle, uncomfortable hesitation manifesting in her back-and-forth.

The therapist seemed to be waiting for it to stop without a scowl or look of disapproval.

"How old are you, Audrey?"

"You have my fucking notes."

"We all change. It's okay. Everything you're experiencing, and feeling, is okay. Mothering two boys. Going through a divorce. Meeting a man who wants to possess you and leave scars on you."

Audrey leaked more tears, but the therapist wasn't finished.

"Choose, Audrey."

Audrey stopped fidgeting. She stilled. Wasn't this life's impetus? Choice.

"You're free. Walk out of my office or stay. Choose. But if you do stay here, own this moment. Be present. And give me what you fear."

Gavin was the only one who had access to what she feared. He. Had. That. No one else. And that was the paradox. She could give Gavin a million moments, but he seemed to want a lifetime of them or a commitment. Both feet.

"I fear regret." Audrey met the therapist's eyes straight on. "I fear making a choice and it being wrong. I fear mediocrity. I fear disappointing my children."

"Fear will hold you captive. It's holding you in its clutches. Gavin's rules, his assertion over certain parts of your life, will only take you so far—"

"I need..."

"What do you need?"

The uniformity all around the room seemed to move, sway, become a mirage. Plain furniture, plain curtains, degrees in frames. Paintings of the ocean perhaps bought by someone else and probably from a catalogue.

"There's not always a concrete solution," the therapist said when Audrey had no answer. "Life means living *with* risk."

"Accepting things."

"Yes, that's part of it. Have you had a vacation lately?"

Audrey laughed.

"I'm serious." The therapist smiled. "Not a vacation for the kids, but somewhere you long to go. Do you enjoy nature?"

"That's your prescription?"

"One of them." She retrieved a travel atlas and then sat next to Audrey on the plain couch. "Turn the pages. Tell me what you know about each state we thumb through and what famous landmarks you'd like to visit."

"This is silly."

"Humor me, Audrey."

By the time they'd finished the exploration, the hour was up. The therapist had made a list, not only of faraway places, but local ones. Audrey committed to Key West and gave serious thought to Tombstone, Arizona, and the Grand Canyon.

"Isn't this distraction?" Audrey asked. "Taking trips? Seeking pleasure?"

"I prefer to call it communing with what you believe in. If it's God, then you reconnect. You put away your phone and the immaterial, and you only look at scenery: skies, mountains, beaches. You don't question it. It's not distraction. It's the moment you're given to either accept or ignore. Confronting feelings is work. Pain teaches us some of life's most important lessons."

No shit. Had the therapist forgotten whom she was speaking to? Audrey knew what kind of lessons pain taught. Wasn't that part of the reason she was here — in the office of a sex therapist? Audrey *needed* pain to teach her lessons.

Pain's lessons were the only ones she wanted to learn.

33

"I had a dream about my mother last night." She often had dreams about her mother, and they always made it seem as if she were still alive.

"Tell me about it."

"Isn't this supposed to be 'sex' therapy?"

"This is therapy, Audrey ... relationships. Sex is one part, not the whole."

Hmmm...

Could've fooled Audrey.

She hadn't had sex for over a year. And after having experienced the awakening of a lifetime, abstinence had made her feel like an addict without a fix. Sex and pain *made her whole* even if they weren't all the pieces of the puzzle.

"You look like you're somewhere else?"

Audrey grinned and focused back on the dream. "Things are always — sorry, not always..." Because there were no such things as *always* and *never*. "When I wake up, it just feels so real that I usually cry. And it's hard to acclimate back to the things that should make me happy."

"What should make you happy?"

"My kids."

"So, because you feel sadness after having a profound, emotional dream, you assume that the love you have for your children isn't satisfying you? You think you're a failure?"

Audrey blinked.

"It sounds silly when I say it out loud, doesn't it?"

Audrey smiled and said, "Yes," rather sheepishly.

"You *are* happy in many facets of your life. I've seen you make much progress since you've been coming here. Define happy for me."

"I can't define it. It's a state of being. A moment."

"Yes. And that's why this dream, or the feelings it momentarily leaves you with, can't change the really important stuff."

After a short pause and a sharp inhale, she felt confident to begin. "My mother had a dollhouse." Audrey smiled, remembering how happy she was every time she saw it. "It was old and made of wood but well cared for, and it once belonged to my grandmother. It had a second story and a set of stairs of course. One wall was missing. It was open on purpose."

Audrey paused, letting that sink in a moment.

"Mom liked to fill it with items she picked up at garage sales. It had such an eclectic mix of things. Tiny playing cards, and I mean miniscule." Audrey gestured. "A little cast iron stove. Plastic beds. A toilet. Area rugs." Audrey laughed. "Trolls she'd probably kept from my old Happy Meals. And..." Audrey chewed on a fingernail. "I still have it ... but I ... I have boys."

"You thought it inappropriate they play with a dollhouse?"

Audrey shrugged. "My husband did. We kept it in the attic after she passed. I still have it up there now ... covered in plastic."

But if it was abandoned...?

Who pulled the strings? Who moved all the little people around? And the furniture? Who made sense of everything?

"Maybe it's time you take it out. Dust it off."

"No, the boys are too ... they wouldn't be interested in it now. I don't know. Maybe Rick..."

"Not for the boys, Audrey. I'm suggesting you take it out for you."

"Grown women don't play with dolls."

"Do grown women get bound and gagged and beaten — because they choose to be dominated? They *choose* to serve."

Audrey felt her eyes enlarge to moons. Her heart rate increased.

"*You choose your happy*. It's not based off someone else's idea of the concept. Not even mine." The therapist scribbled some notes down.

Audrey didn't think she was ready to speak.

"I see I've shocked you."

"I'm just... I never thought of it like that." Audrey swallowed. "The comparison you made. I know submitting was my choice. And I know what some people's perceptions might be about kink. But the dollhouse seemed like something else ... and it's the same."

Audrey was surprised by the invisible rules she still followed. Rules that meant she refused her own happiness and stood in her own way. No one had actually told her playing with the dollhouse would've been silly or stupid. She'd taken strips of supposed judgment and woven together a quilt of conformity.

Her mother had found joy from the house and proudly kept it on display. And Audrey had loved that about her.

Why would it be any different if Audrey did the same?

"Our time is almost up, but I have something I'd like you to think about before the next session. I'm going to read a poem I think you'll appreciate. A client wrote it, and he gave me permission to share it."

The therapist thumbed through her phone, focused on the

screen, and cleared her throat. "'If love was what we wanted it to be, what we set out for it to be — if it was perfect, if we never knew pain — we wouldn't come to know love in its purest, rawest form.

"'The people who say love does not or should not hurt — they're motherfucking liars. The people who say love doesn't live inside scars and welts and bruises ... the ones who say love doesn't roam free inside chains and bounds and ties or collars ... the ones who say it doesn't exist inside a beautiful place like this dungeon—'"

Audrey's loud intake of breath caused the therapist to pause the recital, but then she started again.

"'—they disguise fear with societal blinders. And they live without ever knowing what it's like on the other side of the rainbow.'"

The therapist removed her glasses and set the phone down. "Don't live by your ex-husband's so-called rules. You don't even have to live by Gavin's. And don't invent ones you *think* come from other people, Audrey."

The therapist leaned forward. Her eyes grew wide, and her lips curved. "Break them."

34

"I imagine things I want to say to him and not what you might think."

"I don't have expectations, Audrey," the therapist countered.

"I mean, isn't it weird that after a year of not seeing him, I think about lying next to him and telling him about how Connor's teeth had zero cavities and how Daisy needed a filling and complained about the disgusting toothpaste?"

Audrey had started assisting at a pediatric dental office in St. Petersburg, and she felt the change in atmosphere and cities and houses in every cell of her body. The former office stress, when working for Dr. Marsha, was absent. The new dentist was fabulous with kids.

Many things had informed Audrey's decision to relocate: Dell lived here ... her therapist's main office was in nearby Tampa ... the beautiful beaches ... and she'd talked her dad into moving too. The job was icing on the cake.

"How often do you think about Gavin? I assume the *him* you speak of is Gavin."

"You're asking the wrong question."

"What's the right question?"

"How often do I *not* think about him."

After the accident and the hospital and the standing outside of the dungeon with the gift for Gavin and Michael, Audrey still had never made contact. Neither of them had. It was hard to believe it had been over a year. The ache ever-present in her chest, the love she had for him that felt like it might never die, sometimes made it feel like only weeks had passed.

Kate was a different story, though.

But Audrey didn't want to lead Kate on. And she didn't want any leads to the dungeon. No strings. No temptations. And even though Audrey wasn't bisexual, Kate's infectious personality — her glow, her ease, and her fucking beautiful tits — were all a distraction and a direct line to Gavin and addiction and a lifestyle she couldn't fully immerse herself in.

Maybe Kate and Audrey could still be friends ... the way they had been.

No, they couldn't.

But she missed Kitty Kate.

Missed the nights of getting fixed up and going out. The rides in the cherry-red Mustang. Their sordid talks about men and women.

Kate had said she understood why Audrey had to stop going to Bodhi. But the guilt of initially severing ties with Kate, shortly after Gavin removed Audrey's collar, hadn't left. And the truth was — they *were* friends, whether Audrey could admit it or not. They'd been texting almost daily since Michael had gone into the hospital, talked on the phone too, often bantering like schoolgirls.

Kate wasn't just a friend — she was family. Audrey's mind wandered to a recent exchange...

Kate: Peyton asked me to move in with him.

Audrey: And?

Kate: I said yes. But what if it's a risk?

Audrey: Kate Tracy thinks in terms of risk??

Kate: Brat!

Audrey: Lol

Kate: I guess I still have a little bit of that traditional girl left in me.

Audrey: WTF?

Kate: Why does it feel different if I live with him? It's the same. We're the same. He still wants us both to have play partners. I do too. Except we live together...

Audrey: You fear losing him.

Kate: I never did before. I trust his love. He loves me and only one other.

Kate: You there?

Audrey: Yes. You mean Gavin.

Kate: You said the G word.

Audrey: We're not supposed to be talking about this.

Kate: I break rules.

Audrey: No shit.

Kate: Peyton isn't the only one who loves two people at the same time. Wants them the same...

"Who are you thinking of now?" the therapist asked.

Audrey snapped back to the present and felt her cheeks blush. "Kate."

She loved Kate, but she didn't *love* Kate. Sharing her body would only complicate things. It wouldn't be fair. But what was ever fair in life? Or maybe it was opening herself up to any and every possibility that would complicate things.

Kate: It hasn't changed in all this time. I still want to fuck you. So many things I want to do to you and with you. I can't not tell you anymore. And this will be the only time I mention it.

Audrey: God, Kate.

Kate: I know. I ache for you.

Audrey: I miss you. I miss him. I'm still working things out.

Kate: I love you.

Audrey: It will hurt.

Kate: Being without you hurts too.

Audrey: You have me. We talk all the time.

Kate: I have the pieces you choose to share with me. I want all of you.

"You're still in contact?"

"We text and talk on the phone."

"You haven't seen her? Why?"

"She wants us to be ... *together*."

"And what do you want? Do you want the fantasy, Audrey? Or do you truly yearn for Kate because she's Kate? It's not her gender that's the issue here."

"I want simple. I want Gavin. I'm still in love with him. I want him in my home ... my bed. How can I explain all this to my children? What if I pour my heart out to him and he still doesn't want to be part of my mom life? What if he's moved on?"

"That's too many questions to dissect all at once. Let's go back to Kate. One thing at a time."

Audrey exhaled.

"Would you sleep with Kate if you could manage your emotions and have an open relationship?"

"I don't want to lead her on. I'm not poly. I can't share like that. Can't love like that."

"Can't or don't want to?"

"Both."

"But you want to be with Kate? Sexually?"

Audrey nodded, reminding herself to breathe.

"Say it out loud," the therapist said.

"Why?"

"Have you ever said it out loud?"

"Well, no."

"Then tell me here and now what you feel. Not fantasy. What you really desire."

Audrey folded in on herself, like one of those long beach chairs she used to sit on as a girl. The top and bottom up, meeting in the middle, making a tent, keeping her from the world. She wanted the chair to swallow her excuses.

Even though the sex therapist had probably heard plenty of salacious tales of lust and songs of love inside these four walls, these were still Audrey's thoughts she wanted. Audrey's deepest and most intimate desires. No one owned her thoughts or commanded them.

Only ... Gavin.

"Tell me. Once and for all. You'd be surprised how *hearing* the words will make you feel. This isn't for my benefit."

"I think about her. I always have. From the moment we met, she was so open and free. She flirted with me in a way that never made me feel..." *dirty or shameful but made me feel alive.* Audrey exhaled. "The first time I saw her naked..." *I wanted to taste her breasts, feel them, needed her lips on my skin.* Audrey shivered. "I wanted someone to push me, to tell me what to do to her or for her. Or I wanted Kate to be the one to control me. But we were friends first. We *are* friends. And I feel like I'm..." *a bad person.* "Like there's something wrong with me for wanting her body, for objectifying her."

Except ... she did want to be with Kate because she was Kate.

"Do you love her?"

"Yes," Audrey said without hesitation. "But it's different. It's not what I feel for Gavin."

"Why do you compare one love to another? Nothing *should* feel the same as what you feel for Gavin, but that doesn't mean there isn't room in your heart for two or three or four. You love your children. You love your father. I venture to say you even have love for Dell in there somewhere too. There are four kinds of love, and there's many in our lives who fall into each type. Not just one. Why isn't there room for Kate?"

"There is room for her. I said I love her."

"And fucking Kate will change that?"

"No! Fucking Kate will not change that."

The therapist smirked, looking as if she reached the conclusion she was after. "Maybe you are poly, Audrey."

35

Walking the beach alone at sunset had become a thing. Audrey had been frequenting the west-coast shores ever since she'd moved.

Her ex had the boys, and tonight she had the sunset, the white sand, and the people taking pictures of the disappearing globe. This beach wasn't the one she normally visited. This one was a little farther north and less crowded.

Up ahead, though, there was quite a pack of what looked to be about twenty or twenty-five people posing, doing yoga.

The scene played out like a panorama of a movie — widescreen edition.

Flip-flops in hand, Audrey walked near the water, each step bringing her closer to the group ... closer to their teacher: a man wearing a baseball cap and shorts and a tight-fitting black T-shirt. His arms drew her attention. The short-sleeved cuffs hugged them. His biceps were as large as her thighs and tanned.

Her eyes began to burn. Something familiar settled over her soul, embracing her the way nothing else could. And so ... Audrey glanced away from the man who reminded her of the one person she had never forgotten. Nor ever would. The

picturesque clouds and the gentle breeze needed to take away
the nostalgia seeping through her veins.

She hadn't thought about him in ... what? Hours...

The crowd was older. Baby boomers keeping in shape,
maybe also trying to lose weight. And as she passed directly
behind the teacher, the man with the Tampa Bay Rays cap, it
was the sound of his voice, not his magnificent biceps, that
stopped her in her tracks.

His voice and its timbre made it impossible for those
boomers not to follow him, to hang on every word he said, and it
made it impossible for Audrey to deny the truth of who he was.

He held a pose, but what really struck Audrey was his
posture.

It couldn't be... Teaching fucking yoga?

Like always — and a part of Audrey remained in denial it
was really him — she knew he knew she was there, frozen and
watching him.

"Would you like to join us?" he called out, not turning
around while holding his stance.

Audrey tried to resume walking, but the sand felt like mud.
Her throat had crud stuck in it, and her armpits and palms
began to sweat — not from the early-evening Florida heat.

"First class is free," he said.

Audrey decided he didn't know who she was. He'd merely
sensed a person. The son-of-a-bitch was always on alert.

Keep going. He doesn't know it's you.

But forces outside herself were at work, and even though
she'd managed to take a few steps, she was overcome with the
urge to look at him again. She needed to see his face, not just his
backside. She needed absolute confirmation her mind wasn't
playing tricks.

The man had shifted as well. Left leg bent at a perfect angle,
those same toes in the sand, his right leg stretched behind him,

upper body straight. An arm to the sky. Chest out. His eyes forward...

The eyes were the confirmation.

And as those unmistakable Van Gogh blues locked onto her chestnut browns, a change occurred. Like a man who had once been blinded could suddenly see. The apostle Paul on the road to Damascus.

He blinked.

Broke Sun Salutation.

Blinked.

Fell to his knees. Rubbed his eyes. Retrained them on her. Then blinked again.

He excused himself from his class and took two tentative steps forward, still appearing to be adjusting to a brilliant light he both couldn't bear and needed to save his life.

Audrey took a step backward for each of his forward until she was shin deep in the salty water. Balmy waves caressed her skin.

He wiped a palm over his face, then cleared his throat. "How long has it been?"

"Almost two years," she whispered.

"Audrey," he said and stepped forward, and she stepped back. A wave came and threw her off balance. He caught her wobbly torso on instinct, and the class gasped, then clapped.

They both smiled.

"My God, you look beautiful."

"You look..." She grinned and touched the rim of his cap. "I didn't know you were a fan."

They stood a foot apart now with hands at their sides.

"Keeps the sweat out of my eyes."

"You never had an issue with sweat that I recall."

"No," he said, cocking his head, the blue of his eyes twinkling from the pink-and-purple-and-orange skies, from the light of the disappearing sun. "But this is a different kind of audience."

"Do you still entertain that other audience?" She cleared her throat. "I'm sorry." She shook her head. "I need to go. You have a class."

"Things are... I'm part of my grandchild's life, Audrey. He's my reason now ... after you."

"Don't, Gavin."

"You were always my reason."

"Then why haven't you—?"

"Called? Swept you off your feet? Rode up to your house on a white horse or in a limousine with a rose between my teeth?"

"You have nice teeth." She smiled. "And I don't remember you being this funny."

He glanced away, and when he looked back, his face was placid. His Adam's apple bobbed. "I'm not a husband."

"I have to go," she said but didn't mean it. Therapy sessions and living again — really living — had taught her not to walk away from difficult conversations. "No. You know what? I don't. I'll wait. Finish your class, then we can talk."

"A switch now?" He raised an eyebrow. "Giving me orders." He grinned, then returned to the yoga.

She watched him with his students. Watched those fucking arms and hands. The way he carried himself told her everything there was to know about him. It didn't matter if she'd just found out he was a baseball fan.

Gavin Sellers:

confident

daring

absolute

fearless

not a husband...

"Walk with me," he said several minutes later, after he'd

dismissed the class.

He removed the cap and wiped his forehead with his shirt, exposing a faint trail of hair on his abdomen, and then he took her shoes and his hat and tossed them onto the sand.

"Hey!"

"We'll come back for them. And I want to hold your hand."

Her body stilled. She swallowed that fucking lump of mud and shut off the valve of tears threatening to leak. As he laced his fingers through hers, her entire body turned to Jell-O. She hadn't expected to feel such a profound sense of relief from the contact.

The universe spoke via their hands and fingerprints and skin — and this time, she would pay better attention and listen to what it said.

"You made amends with your son?"

"We built a bridge. We mostly have holidays and birthdays together. Michael continues to have his limits."

She laughed.

"Why is that funny?"

"Because you, Gavin. Don't you see the irony? You live in a world that thrives on limits."

He shook his head and smiled. "Do you still play?"

"Are we doing this right now? Total honesty?"

"I said I wanted to give you that when we met, 'open communication,' but I kept parts of myself from you. I was selfish."

"I haven't ... what we had ... what we did together..."

"It's okay, baby girl. Take your time."

"When I left it wasn't because I stopped loving you." Audrey sighed, and Gavin brushed a thumb across her cheek and smiled.

"All along ... I was safe with you. I should've trusted you that day. But I panicked. And everything we'd been doing suddenly felt extreme — especially compared to my mom life. I started being afraid of having it all and balancing the two. But I miss it. I miss you. And I haven't found or searched for anyone who..." She trailed off, the damn mud thickening in her throat again.

"I dabble but mostly outside the dungeon. I gave it to Peyton."

"Gave what to Peyton?"

"The dungeon. I own it. He runs it. I rarely play there."

"Why?"

"I want other things too. And some people in the lifestyle, like you said, they want both — a sense of vanilla with their kink. I needed a home, a place my grandson could visit. I lived out of the fucking place for too long. It was never supposed to be where I slept. What I set out to do at Bodhi, I did ... we did." And she knew he was thinking of Harper. "I just came to realize I didn't need to keep experiencing it the way I'd originally envisioned in order to be satisfied."

Gavin paused and looked at the skies. The sun was gone, but it's light hadn't quite dimmed. "What do you want, Audrey? I've wished to ask you that question for a long time. I thought you wanted a man who could give you everything: flowers, baseball games, family dinners."

"Turns out you like baseball games."

He grinned, but then as quickly as his smile had appeared, it faded. "I didn't want to hurt you again."

"I found out, or I accepted, no man can give me everything, Gavin."

"I just want you, Audrey." He closed his eyes, squeezed her palm, and when he opened them, he said, "I want to meet your family."

"Jesus, Gavin."

"Yeah, Jesus may have had a lot to do with it."

She laughed.

"Did giving the dungeon to Peyton have anything to do with

... well, I mean did you feel ashamed of the lifestyle after the baby came? Because of Michael? Did you think what you were doing there was wrong?"

"No. I don't. It's not wrong. You know that in your heart." He slid a finger across her chin, and she nodded in agreement, leaning her face into his caress. "But I do have to respect my son. And while he can't dictate how I live my life or give me ultimatums, I do allow this concession because I want him in my life and because I know I can be fulfilled without the everyday or every single weekend activity. I wasn't happy there when you met me. The dungeon had become static, and pushing you became an extreme sport I needed to excel at."

"But you ... what about Peyton? You still—?"

"I see Peyton," he said, and Audrey heard what that meant in his voice, saw what it meant in his eyes. "I know you speak to Kate."

"We don't discuss the G word."

"I haven't had... I haven't collared anyone, Audrey."

"I still have it."

"I want to put it on you."

"This is too fast."

"It feels like a day hasn't gone by. Kate only stays quiet because I beg her to, Audrey. She knows how much I love you."

Audrey couldn't feel her legs. Goose bumps ran through her body. Warmth spread to her head, her cheeks.

"It felt like a million have gone by. But being with you now makes it seem like it all happened yesterday," she said, her eyes reflecting her *I love you* ... or she hoped. "What if we hadn't run into each other today?"

"What if the apostle Paul hadn't been on the road to Damascus?"

Fuck. Fuck. Fuck. Gavin fucking Sellers. How could he have known she'd thought about that?

Audrey shivered.

He touched her cheek. "This feels like old times."

"I don't want old times. I want new."

"What we have ... our connection ... it feels old and new. I'm still me." He smiled wickedly. "We ... trying to balance a home life, especially one with kids, and be in the community — it's new for you. The most important thing to remember is that we need *this* too." He lifted their bound hands. "We need transparency *and* balance."

"What if something happens? Even like this?" She glanced at their intertwined fingers — the wish to hold his hand through fire, while climbing mountains, across deserts, never stronger. "What if I...?"

"You mean..." Without releasing her palm, he reached up and caressed her ear, her jawline, then her bottom lip. His eyes were full of love and piety, godlikeness. She knew she'd pleased him. "What if you break open?"

But she'd already been broken.

And she'd opened.

She'd healed.

Her fears weren't something she needed to run from any longer. And this man was the ultimate partner, *not everything*, but one she could walk alongside, holding hands — ready to safely explore whatever else was in store: sexually, emotionally, spiritually.

God ... the possibilities seemed endless. More than a dream or an adventure. Their collision seemed foreordained and necessary. Then and now.

"Hey," he began, and she kept her eyes locked on his. "I don't have all the answers. But I want to ask the questions."

And they were already racing through Audrey's mind...

How would he cane her inside the four walls of her bedroom? How could she keep quiet when he burned her, sucked her nipples to the point of pain, and whispered disgusting but beautiful songs of ownership into her waiting ears? Would he still long to share her body with others? Did he still need to watch her take other men's cocks? Did he still want her to? Did she? And what about Kate and Peyton? Did he still...?

"Audrey..." he said, a smile in his eyes and on his lips. Gavin could still read her thoughts. Anticipate her needs.

"Me too," she said in reply to his previous statement.

"We'll figure it out, baby girl. I promise we'll have open communication. Completely. We'll talk about what we want and need. Nothing is off the table."

"Including baseball?"

"Including baseball." He smiled.

They started to walk again, and after they'd strolled ... maybe a quarter mile, Gavin tugged on her hand. "Audrey?"

"What is it?" She came to a stop. "Gavin..." she said and looked around the beach.

He'd begun to lift his tee, and at first, she'd stupidly thought it was hardly the place to take off a shirt — feeling moonstruck threw logic out the window. But any and all thoughts of what he might do ceased once she locked onto a tattoo on his chest above and across his left pectoral muscle.

"Darcy's work?" she asked in a strangled whisper.

"Yeah."

He looked pained in the most beautiful way possible. Open and exposed, not just bare-chested, his heart beating on the outside of his skin.

"Touch me, Audrey."

Sucking in a breath, the sound in her lungs stronger than the tide, she placed her fingers on his skin, grazing the colorful ink of the tattoo.

Rings of fire around wheels of chariots ... angels with wings as drivers.

He closed his eyes as she circled the images with the tips of her fingers.

"So I never forget," he choked out on an exhale, his eyes still closed.

Audrey flattened her palm over the symbol and pressed her lips to his — tasting salt, sweat, and pure Gavin — their tongues exchanging redemption and forgiveness, lust and temptation ... love.

Taking her in his arms, Gavin intensified the kiss, minus the bruising force Audrey remembered. This kiss was different. Gavin tasted like love. Smelled like love. Felt like love. All four kinds.

Fuck society. Fuck the standards that locked people into closets.

Gavin and Audrey had always been *love*. And they would always be love. Because love *bears all things, believes all things, hopes all things, endures all things.*

And because ... this man owned this woman, not only her body, but her soul, spirit, and heart.

Audrey knew in this moment it was Gavin who'd returned. *Don't come back to me unless it's with both feet.* Gavin had been the one who'd decided each of them could have a foot in both worlds. One foot planted where people drove minivans, attended movies, and baseball practices ... and the other foot in the darkness of the light. A place where acceptance and experimentation and being whole meant more than following rules.

Gavin and Audrey made their own rules.

Husband and wife were only titles.

In their world, it was those *other* titles that held weight, assigned power, created trust, honored commitment.

I do, sir.

Good girl.

EPILOGUE

Gavin and Audrey made plans to visit Peyton's downtown condo near the dungeon on a Saturday night around 8 p.m.

Candles placed on counters and shelves and tables lit the living room and adjacent kitchen, creating shadow puppets on the walls. Toys of the adult kind lay strewn across the bar top — tools some might've called devices of torture and others ... every girl with an imagination called fun.

Peyton had been the one who'd come to the door, his sun-kissed hair grazing his shoulders, wearing a pair of board shorts and a smile. He also sported one of those skin-tight athletic shirts ... as did Gavin. Both men patted each other on the back and said hello, Gavin's arms straining and flexing with the gesture. But his muscles weren't just a display — those biceps stood for security and warmth — the best Audrey had ever known.

Kate, looking comfortable in a hot-pink robe over what Audrey assumed was a naked body, stood next to a bottle of open red and a selection of vibrators.

Catching up happened first. A few tears were shed by the girls. Hugs exchanged. Glasses of water offered instead of wine.

This would mark the first time they'd all been together in the same room and at the same time, only the four of them, alone, since the split and the make-up.

"We made ground rules," Peyton said after about thirty minutes of laughing and chatting had passed, clearing the tension-filled air. "I don't have to wait for his commands to do something, but Gavin will lead. Everyone will defer to him tonight."

Audrey's palms had already started perspiring when Gavin took hold of one, keeping it safe in his grasp, making her remember why she'd agreed with the arrangement they'd discussed for the night.

She trusted him with every fiber of her being. Trusted herself more.

"Does anyone else want wine?" Kate lifted the bottle.

"How many glasses have you had, Kitty?" Gavin asked, and Kate held up a finger.

"I want you both sober," he said, wiping the pad of his thumb across Kate's bottom lip.

Audrey sucked in a breath — it was fucking happening — as Gavin undid the knot on Kate's robe and opened the lapels.

Audrey had been wrong. She wasn't naked.

But the only things Kate had on were a black thong and fading bruises on her tits and inner thighs ... maybe more on her back too.

"You've been a bad kitty?" Gavin tugged on her nipple.

"Yes," she breathed out and smiled.

Peyton grinned too, his brown eyes growing darker by the second, as his best friend and sometimes lover tweaked the nipple of his other lover, his partner, his collared submissive.

The women faced one another from less than a foot apart, as did the men. They formed a square. Audrey couldn't tear her gaze from Gavin's fingers or Kate's breasts.

"Audrey," Gavin said, and her eyes followed the sound of his voice. "Kiss her. She wants you so badly. Have you kissed each other before?"

They both answered together. "A little peck," and, "No, sir."

All four of them smiled.

Moving behind Audrey, Gavin slipped off her jacket, and then he lifted her shirt over her head. Leaning forward, he put his lips at her ear and said, "Kiss her, baby girl," then he nudged her closer to Kate.

Inches separated the women now, their breasts the only things touching. Audrey's tiny peaks were still covered by a lacy bra. Kate's huge tits were bare and bruised, nipples pink, the sounds of their breathing labored, each waiting for the delicious consummation.

The moment Audrey touched her lips to Kate's, Kate purred.

Their tongues mingled, wet and warm and full of passion. Hot breath clouded their jitters and any leftover fears. As they explored — slow and sensual, loving and proud — their moans and purrs grew louder, desperate, and their centers began to grind against each other as their hands roamed. Audrey latched onto Kate's thigh, rubbing her sex over her skin without shame, needing to sate the motherfucking need. Now. Tonight.

"Fuck," Kate groaned into Audrey's mouth and squirmed.

Gavin, still behind Audrey, his heat reminding her he was never far, slid his hands over the front of her shoulders and slipped them into her bra, flicking her nipples with the pads of his thumbs.

"Fuck ... you're such a good girl, Audrey. My Audrey," Gavin whispered with barely any breath, and Audrey moaned against Kate's lips.

Peyton wiggled his fingers between Gavin's chest and Audrey's shoulder blades and unclasped her bra. After removing the garment, he bent and sucked on one of Audrey's nipples, getting some of Gavin's fingers in the process.

As Audrey broke from Kate's lips to watch, her body trembling, her knees buckling, Gavin said, "I have you, baby girl," then she leaned into his embrace and relaxed. "Kate, suck my girl too."

Gavin and Audrey couldn't take their eyes from Peyton and Kate's devotion, observing with keen interest as they sucked and licked and nibbled Audrey's tiny breasts and perfect nipples, every bit of her supple mounds of flesh disappearing into their wet mouths.

"Yeah." Gavin grunted and pulled on Audrey's hair. "You like that, baby girl? You like getting sucked? Teased? Played with?" He had her in his infamous chokehold, his forearm clutching her neck while two fingers of his other hand lay pressed in the hollow beneath his collar. "Answer me."

"Mmm ... yes," she sputtered.

"Tell them." He put more pressure on her throat, yanking on the silver chain, and then he bit her shoulder hard. She knew it would leave a mark ... and then a bruise.

"I like it," she cried, then coughed.

"What?" he relaxed the hold he had on her throat, and she gasped for air. "What do you like?"

Audrey knew Gavin would push for everything he'd ever wanted tonight — not just her body, but her soul, her words, her rights — and she wanted him to take it all ... break her and put her back together.

Except ... this didn't feel like being broken. It felt like being molded and loved, completed.

"I like being sucked. Oh, fuck..." she said, and Peyton and Kate both bit down on her fat, plump nipples. "Please ... please, sir. Please."

"Get her pants off and bend her over the arm of the couch, Peyton," Gavin ordered, and Peyton happily complied.

Once her ass was up and feet were on the floor, Gavin kicked Audrey's legs open, and then he parted her butt cheeks and folds, inspecting his slave and showing Peyton and Kate what he would gift them tonight.

"Mine," he growled and stroked Audrey nape to tailbone. "Over here, Kate. Feed her your tits."

The moment Kate got into position, knees on the floor, resting to the left of the couch arm, Audrey began to feast, licking and sucking Kate's tits like she was starved for them.

"Holy fuck," Kate giggled. "God, that feels good."

"Peyt, I want your cock there too. Stand by your Kitty and fill my girl's little mouth until she gags on cock and tit."

Already stroking his hard dick, Peyton joined Kate and fought for entry.

"Yeah." Gavin yanked on Audrey's hair until she yelped over the flesh fighting for her mouth: breasts pliant and soft, dick smooth and hard.

"Feed her. Yeah. My good girl is hungry. She wants to be fed and bruised. She wants to be used. Don't you, Audrey?"

Audrey whimpered and moaned while Gavin continued pulling at the roots of her hair, making her eyes water and her body sing. And then came the fulfillment of the promise: delicious, delectable pain.

A paddle ... always his favorite tool.

Gavin delivered a nice swift slap to her ass with his thin wooden paddle, and then another. Left cheek, then right, in perfect tandem.

"Don't you dare stop sucking them," he said, slapping her again and again and again. "No biting either."

Drool slid down her chin, the sounds she made indicating she never wanted it to end.

"Fuck..." he hissed as the grain struck her again and again. "You need this, baby girl?" Gavin massaged her ass cheeks with his strong hands.

Tongue busy licking Kate's nipples, Audrey moaned her approval, her joy, her ecstasy. Then Peyton said, "Smell Katy Kitten." His juice-soaked fingers were under Audrey's nose. "My fingers were just in her cunt, Audrey." He painted her swollen upper lip with pussy. "You can smell all of us now ... even Gav through his jeans." He laughed.

"Four more lashes," Gavin said, a strain in his voice. "Then we fuck. All of us. We'll all fuck you tonight, Audrey. No more waiting. Each of us will finally have a piece of you."

And then, he counted as he rained pleasure across her ass. Everything this meant to him was apparent in each syllable that followed.

"One. Two. Three. Four."

He dropped the paddle, then swatted Audrey's cheeks with the palm of his hand. "Put on your dildo, Kate, and lie on the couch."

While they waited for her to prepare, Gavin had Audrey stand, and then he gripped Peyton's rock-hard length and pumped him while she watched. Peyton cupped Audrey's pussy and fucked Gavin's fist. All three of them grunting, fighting for air, filling with a balloon of lust she hoped would never pop.

Audrey no longer came between the men — although she stood between them — as Gavin and Peyton shared a kiss Audrey could feel lighting a magnificent fire inside her muscles and bones.

She didn't come between them ... she joined them. They would all join.

"Okay," Kate said, chest glistening, nipples hard. A huge, life-like-looking cock was strapped to her body, pointing up and ready.

"Isn't she pretty, baby girl," Gavin said, Peyton's cock still secure in his palm. "Isn't Kate beautiful?"

"Yes, sir."

"Thank her for accepting this gift."

"Thank you, Kate," Audrey said, and both girls had a few tears streaming down their faces now. "You're beautiful. Thank you for accepting my gift."

Audrey's body was in an upheaval. Like nothing she'd felt before. Emotions coming and going. Stomach swirling. Head burning with fever.

"God..." Kate moaned as Gavin guided Audrey toward her, then placed her on the faux cock.

He spread open her folds again, baring her clit and hole for them all to esteem. "Your gift."

"Yes," Kate hissed, and Peyton slipped his fingers between the women's bodies and began to play with their clits.

"Take her all the way," Gavin whispered to Audrey, and she relaxed. "Take her cock. Yeah ... like that. Fuck her, baby girl."

After Audrey rode Kate — up, down, fast, slow — for a few minutes, she then bent forward and sucked on Kate's tits while Gavin started to finger Audrey's asshole, preparing it, stretching it, filling it with lube.

Peyton fucked his own fist, keeping the fingers of his other hand between the women, fondling them, urging them on with filthy words and a sly smile.

"Audrey," Gavin said and removed what felt like three fingers from her asshole. "It's time. You'll be filled with all of us tonight. Do you want this?"

Each word he uttered ... a dream she'd dreamed long ago.

"Yes," she choked out.

And now she trusted the love enough to follow through with what had always been much more than fantasy. It was expression, acceptance, living life to the fullest this side of reality.

She'd become someone who walked without fear and loved without boundaries.

"Sir," Audrey breathed out the moment the tip of his dick breached her asshole. She tried not to rock her clit against Kate's body or Peyton's hand. Tried not to objectify Kate's breasts or imagine the taste of Peyton's dick. Tried not to explode with an orgasm threatening to crumble the walls of her uterus. "Please..."

"Don't you dare fucking come yet." He thrust himself inside her hole to the hilt — never any preamble with Gavin.

"Fuck, man," Peyton said.

"Open your mouth, Audrey," Gavin ordered, and Peyton put his tip there. "Slow at first. Yes?"

"Yes," they all agreed, finding a rhythm soon after the word left their mouths.

Three people claiming a hole. Three connections. Three different types of love.

Audrey made sure to feel each of them together *and* separately. Physically, yes, but spiritually too. The connection they shared hadn't faded with the lost time. Prolonging the orgy had been worth the wait.

Everything Audrey had struggled against for years, and finally accepted, had readied her for being open tonight. Heart and body and mind. The love they all had for each other pulsated through her body via their thrusts, their cocks, their whispers, their sighs.

The love may have varied in intensity and type between the four, but it wasn't lacking.

Nothing was missing.

Kate brushed away Audrey's tears and mouthed *I love you* while Audrey nodded in understanding of their quad accord.

"It's okay, Audrey," Gavin said as she shook a little in his grasp. "My precious girl. We all have you, want you ... care for you."

"I love you, Gavin," Audrey said after releasing Peyton for a moment from her mouth, but she spoke for the benefit of each pair of ears, full of the tears and energy she harnessed. "Please, Master." She was a cable connector, electricity passing between her, outstretching to the other three.

"Yes, beautiful girl," he said.

And Audrey released, crying and coming, sagging and moaning ... each hole filled to the brim. Two overtaken by friends. The third sealed by her Dominant, her partner — the man who wasn't a husband but an owner, a protector, a savior.

Filled.

Loved.

Contented.

In the moment, Audrey stayed.

Happy.

Not chasing anything that would fade.

Not afraid.

Not dreaming.

In love with Gavin.

Room in her heart for others.

The four of them would fuck all night — that was what they'd planned on doing: laughing, talking, eating, and fucking ... maybe sleeping — and then Gavin and Audrey would go home in the morning. To her home. Their home. The one they shared with her sons. Not pretending. They could do whatever they chose.

And tonight, they'd chosen to initiate Audrey into ... not hedonism, but a circle. They'd chosen to use Audrey's body as a vessel. And tonight, she'd chosen to be the sacrifice. The reason. The final piece of the fucking puzzle.

They all fit together — the way it was meant to be.

Peyton would dominate Gavin (occasionally).

Kate would love Peyton (always) and Audrey (a fucking lot).

And Gavin would only give his heart and soul and mind to Audrey. He would only share her with his two best friends (mmm ... probably).

The collar signified she was Gavin's alone, his to do with as he pleased. And right now, Gavin and Audrey were beyond pleased because both of their feet would remain wherever the fuck they planted them ... so long as their toes touched solid earth.

They were grounded in love and kink. They made their own fucking rule book.

The End

————

Signup for A.R. Hadley's newsletter and receive the FREE novella Wash My Sins!
Stay abreast of new releases and contests.

https://www.arhadley.com/newsletter

ALSO BY A.R. HADLEY

BODHI

THE FLYAWAYS

THE TRUTH IN THE LIE

MOONLIGHT DRIVE

ACKNOWLEDGMENTS

Jesus Christ. This book...

This was one of those stories that grabbed me by the throat (no pun intended) and wouldn't let go. It came to me hard and fast (pun intended), and I couldn't spit the words fast enough.

Nope, my mom hasn't read it.

And some lovers of God and Jesus may never understand it, or they'll pass judgment. And that's okay. This is life.

I'm glad you took the time to consider it, and I hope the emotions were something you tasted and touched and could see ... not just read.

My editor, Monica Black, is a Godsend. She has the right words at the right times, not just in the margins of the manuscript. And she gave me a hell of a lot of fabulous suggestions.

Kate Heywood is a friend I never expected to meet. I suppose that's how great friendships start... She pushes me, makes me better, and she's really funny. And she campaigned for the name of the book. And won!

Thank you to the parentheses. I used them a lot in this novel because I'm weird and I can.

Thank you to another Kate and Audrey for having been beautiful and strong, for doing things in what some have called a "man's world" when it wasn't popular to do so, like wearing pants and loving who you wanted to.

It takes a village! Thank you, friends and bloggers, for reading and sharing. Thank you, Najla, for making my *first* man cover and doing it beyond what I could've imagined. Thank you, Cassie and Devon, for proofing. Thank you, Sarah, Kate, April, Renee, Sierra, and Mellie, for advising and critiquing! Thank you, Leslie, for being a champion for ALL writers, and for looking for any remaining pesky little typos!

There are a few nods in the book as well — to friends and authors and people I think are pretty freaking amazing! Did you catch any?

Big hugs and kisses to you all!

And now, I leave you with one wish: when you feel repressed or suppressed from the burden of society's "rules," follow the advice of Audrey's therapist:

"Break them!"

...within reason, of course. I mean, we're not talking about robbing banks or anything. *wink*

ABOUT THE AUTHOR

A.R. Hadley writes imperfectly perfect sentences by the light of her iPhone.
She loves the ocean.
Chocolate.
Her children.
And Cary Grant.
She annoys those darling little children by quoting lines from *Back to the Future*, but despite her knowledge of eighties and nineties pop culture, she was actually meant to live alongside the Lost Generation after the Great War and write a mediocre novel while drinking absinthe with Hemingway. Instead, find her sipping unsweet tea near a garden as she weaves fictional tales of love and connection amid reality.

https://www.arhadley.com

facebook.com/arhadleywriter
twitter.com/ARHadleyWriter
instagram.com/arhadleywriter
bookbub.com/authors/a-r-hadley
amazon.com/A.R.-Hadley/e/B01J7WHH16